CATHERINE FARNES

JOURNEY FORTH™

Greenville, South Carolina

Library of Congress Cataloging-in-Publication Data

Farnes, Catherine, 1964-
  The slide / by Catherine Farnes.
      p. cm.
Sequel to: Over the divide.
Summary: When her father reappears after years away, Taren agrees to
go backpacking with her church youth group as an escape from her
emotional and spiritual struggles.
  ISBN: 1-57924-967-1 (perfect bound paperback : alk. paper)
  [1. Backpacking—Fiction. 2. Fathers—Fiction. 3. Christian life—
Fiction.] I. Title.
  PZ7.F238265SI 2003
  [Fic]—dc21

                                                              2003002309

The Slide

Cover and Design by TJ Getz
Composition by Melissa Matos

© 2003 BJU Press
Greenville, SC 29614

Printed in the United States of America

ISBN 1-57924-967-1

15   14   13   12   11   10   9   8   7   6   5   4   3   2   1

In loving memory of
Carolyn Jean Farnes
August 20, 1943–July 29, 2002

Books by Catherine Farnes

The Rivers of Judah Series
  Rivers of Judah
  Snow
  Out of Hiding
  The Way of Escape

Over the Divide
The Slide

Contents

Chapter 1 1

Chapter 2 5

Chapter 3 14

Chapter 4 20

Chapter 5 27

Chapter 6 34

Chapter 7 41

Chapter 8 48

Chapter 9 54

Chapter 10 61

Chapter 11 69

Chapter 12 76

Chapter 13 81

Chapter 14 92

Chapter 15 98

Chapter 16 105

Chapter 17 110

Chapter 18 117

Chapter 19 124

Of all the people on the planet that I could have run into at Rimrock Mall on a Saturday afternoon, it was so like my life that Ezra Adams would be the one. He spotted me eating an ice-cream cone and invited himself over to join me.

It wasn't that Ezra wasn't decent looking. He was. And it wasn't even that I didn't like him as a person. I did. It was just that he had become such a clone of his father—Mom's pastor and mine—since his mom had died that I couldn't relate to him anymore.

Add to that my own confusion over my father's recent reappearance into our lives after nine years of absence . . . Ezra Adams and I had nothing in common.

"How are you doing, Taren?" he asked me as he sat across from me at my tiny table for two. "I haven't seen you except Sunday mornings since school let out."

"I know." I shrugged. "Things have been kind of crazy for me lately."

He nodded slowly. "My dad has been spending quite a bit of time with your parents."

"Great," I said.

"We've missed you at youth group," he said, obviously adequately convinced by my icy tone that I didn't appreciate the direction he'd hoped to take the conversation. "If you come tonight," he added, "you can still get in on our summer trip."

That almost intrigued me. "Where are you guys going?"

"Lower Aero Lake. Upper Aero Lake. Lady of the Lake. Sky Top Lakes. Sky Top Glacier."

I smiled. I couldn't help it. "So let me guess. Based on the eager look on your face, these are not places a person can drive to?"

"Nope," he said. "We're going to hike in with an outfitter friend of my dad's."

The fact that Pastor Adams had an outfitter friend didn't surprise me. Neither did Ezra's obvious excitement about the upcoming adventure. My own interest, however, did.

But I had the soon-to-be-a-sophisticated-junior image to uphold and absolutely no desire to go anywhere—even if it did sound interesting—with the church youth group.

"I hate hiking." I stood up, tossed my unfinished cone into a nearby trash can, and turned away from Ezra. "See you."

"Yup," he said behind me.

After two hours of wandering the mall with no money and without running into anyone else, I decided I might as well head home.

"Oh, Taren," Mom said before I'd even gotten fully through the front door. She smiled up at me from the floor where she was kneeling to change my two-year-old cousin's diaper. "I'm glad you're back. I wanted to tell you before he gets here that I invited your father for dinner again. I hope that's—"

"Actually, Mom," I said, suddenly thankful that I'd run into Ezra Adams, "I thought I might go to youth group tonight. They're planning their big backpacking trip and—"

"I know," she said. "Okay."

"I'm sure my father will understand I've got places I'd rather be." I hurried by my mother and ran up the stairs and into my room before she could open her mouth. Sometimes I hated the way she never seemed to know what to say to me anymore, but at other times, times like this one, it did work to my advantage.

The last thing I wanted to do was sit through another Jesus-would-want-you-to-give-your-father-a-chance lecture.

My father hadn't worried about what Jesus would have wanted him to do when he'd packed up and left Mom and me when I was just seven. Or when it was my birthday or Christmas or my next birthday or Christmas again or the birthday after that, and he didn't even call or send a card.

Tears burned my eyes as I slid cold metal hanger after cold metal hanger across the cold metal closet bar looking for something, anything, appropriate to wear to youth group. Most of the clothes hanging in front of me had been bought during the six months since Dad had moved back to town, and they weren't particularly modest. The shorter skirts and sweaters made me feel cold as I looked at them now, but I did find a nice long sweater and a new jean skirt. The skirt was shorter than Mom would have tolerated before we'd gotten into all this conflict about my father, but she'd begun to selectively ignore some of the things we could fight about in favor of focusing on the things that she thought would matter most in the eternal scheme of my life. At least that's how she'd been explaining herself to me. The skirt was no shorter than some of the ones that I'd seen some of the other girls from church wearing at school, so I figured it would be okay.

Besides, Pastor Adams and the kids who really cared about me would probably be so relieved to see me at a church function of my own free will that they wouldn't care if my skirt wasn't perfect. They knew how confusing my life had been lately.

Even though I knew that I had decided to go for all the wrong reasons—I was angry at my mother, and I did not want to eat another meal with my father—I felt as if I might be doing the right thing.

That was a feeling I hadn't given myself a whole lot of opportunity to enjoy recently.

As I walked out the door just in time to ignore my father as he pulled his silver pickup into our driveway and waved at me, I remembered something Mom had said to me the first time we'd fought about whether or not we should keep seeing my father.

"I understand that you want to run right now, Taren. I don't blame you. I can't even imagine how you must be feeling."

I tensed at the memory that I had interrupted her then to shout that that, at least, was one thing she was right about. *Nobody can imagine how I'm feeling.*

"You can run from me," Mom had continued, absorbing my comment without comment, "and you can run from your father, but you can't run from God."

Then she'd quoted some of Psalm 139 to me. Verses I already knew because I'd memorized them as a child in Sunday school when Mrs. Adams had still been alive and had taught us.

"Whither shall I go from thy spirit? or whither shall I flee from thy presence? If I ascend up into heaven, thou art there: if I make my bed in hell, behold, thou art there. If I take the wings of the morning, and dwell in the uttermost parts of the sea; Even there shall thy hand lead me, and thy right hand shall hold me. If I say, Surely the darkness shall cover me; even the night shall be light about me. Yea, the darkness hideth not from thee; but the night shineth as the day: the darkness and the light are both alike to thee. For thou hast possessed my reins: thou hast covered me in my mother's womb."

It certainly did seem as though plenty of darkness had covered my life.

As for all the rest of it?

That remained to be seen.

In the meantime, a week into and out of Lone Elk Lake and wherever else Ezra's father's outfitter friend dared to take a somewhat obnoxious group of city teenagers sounded like the perfect distraction. The perfect excuse to steal away, even if only for a little while, from Mom and my father and my own anger at my own anger . . . and all the other jagged shards that now took the place of what had once upon a time been my fairly decent and put-together life.

CHAPTER **02**

The church sanctuary smelled just the same as it always did. Like a new wool coat. Only it smelled even more so like that now that it was empty. I didn't think I'd ever had the room to myself before, and I wasn't sure I liked the experience. Sitting alone near the back waiting for the other kids to arrive, the smell and the place surrounded me, both familiar and alien.

I'd come early because I'd been in a hurry to get out of the house. I'd come in quietly because I didn't want Pastor Adams or any of his youth staff who might be in the building to hear me and rush in to greet me. I'd sat at the back of the sanctuary because I felt as if I shouldn't be getting any closer to the big wood cross on the wall behind the plain wood pulpit.

The stillness. The smell. The cross.

It all began to unnerve me after about ten seconds, and I hurried out of the sanctuary and would have kept going right out the front door except that Ezra and his father walked up just then and blocked my way.

It was coincidence, I was sure, but it felt more like a setup.

"Hey, Taren," Pastor Adams said as he extended his hand to me. "It's great to see you."

"You too," I managed.

"Decided to get in on some hiking?" Ezra grinned.

"Maybe," I said.

5

"It's going to be a fantastic trip." Pastor Adams placed his hand on my shoulder and directed me toward the stairway and into the youth room at the bottom, talking the whole way about all the places and things and animals we would see.

"Well," I said as I sat on a cold metal chair, "anything would be better than being home right now."

I regretted my words as soon as I'd said them because they'd evoked that familiar look of compassion on the pastor's face. I could feel a Taren-you-know-God-loves-you-even-though-your-life-is-confused-right-now-and-if-there's-anything-we-can-do-to-help lecture coming on like an early first snow. I started to say something else in an attempt to keep the inevitable from happening, but the pastor spoke more quickly.

"Taren," he said, plainly and matter-of-factly, "think about where you would be if Christ had been unwilling to forgive you."

No mushy sympathy there. That was for sure.

Even though the pastor had spoken the words kindly enough, and even though his concern was obvious in his expression and in his tone of voice, I couldn't help feeling that he believed much of my confusion and misery—if not all of it—was my own fault.

As if *I'd* caused my father to leave Mom and me.

As if *I'd* asked him to come back into my life after nine years when it had taken me almost seven and a half of those years to quit hoping he'd come back.

As if I should be glad that my father had found faith in God and the strength to come back and try to make things right.

People said hi to me and the meeting started, but I barely noticed because of all the noise in my own head. Part of me agreed with Pastor Adams and part of me rose up in defense of my choices as the victim of a lousy situation.

I hadn't resolved anything within myself when Pastor Adams started talking about the upcoming trip at the conclusion of his Bible study, but I forced myself to pay attention to him.

If I was going to decide to go on this trip, I wanted to know what to expect.

"We'll be a day getting to Cooke Pass and getting our packs ready," Pastor Adams told us. "Then we'll be a week on the trail including hiking out and the drive home. Nine of you can come this time along with Mr. and Mrs. Emery and me. If more of you are interested, we can try to plan a second trip." He leaned forward with his wrists on his knees. "So who's coming?"

Ezra lifted his hand. So did four or five other boys.

Pastor Adams turned his attention to the girls.

"I can't go," one of them said. "I have basketball camp."

"I've got cheerleading camp," another said.

"I don't do the camping thing," a third said.

At least she was honest.

"Will we be able to wash our hair?" the new girl beside me, Madison Petrik, wanted to know.

"With lake water," Ezra said. "But it's cold."

"I don't care about that," Madison said. "As long as I can wash my hair." She shrugged. "I guess I'll go."

Some of the boys nudged each other and laughed. "Like she'll be able to carry a backpack," Payne Chisholm whispered.

Either that boy's mother had had foreknowledge of the kind of clown her son would grow up to be when she chose his name, I reflected as I watched Pastor Adams reprimand Payne with a stern look, or fifteen years of being called "Payne the Pain" had taken their toll.

Madison smiled and told Payne the Pain that he needn't worry about her. She could do anything he or any of the rest of his buddies could do.

But I had to wonder.

She was tiny and thin.

I was thin enough, but not tiny, so if Madison figured she could carry a backpack up the side of a mountain, I guessed I could too. "I'll go," I said to Pastor Adams.

None of the boys laughed and nudged one another about that.

They did high-five one another, though, when Rachel Moore raised her hand. Rachel was and always had been the most popular girl in youth group and at school and everywhere else. She was gorgeous, it was true, but she was also a decent human being. All the boys tried to get her to date them even though everyone knew that she didn't bother with that "nonsense" because God had called her to missionary work in Eastern Europe, and she intended to let nothing get in the way of that. It was a little strange for someone our age to be so completely focused on something so different and far away and spiritual, but we all respected Rachel for it. None of us had any doubt that we'd be e-mailing her in Prague or somewhere not too long after her graduation from the Bible college she already knew she'd be going to even though she was still just a sophomore.

I realized as I watched her take her permission slip—the last one—from Pastor Adams that I envied her.

Rachel Moore had everything, and she had it together.

But then her father hadn't done what my father had done. My father had been in church with Mom and me nearly every Sunday since he'd moved back to town. (And Mom wonders why I'm not getting anything out of the services!) Rachel's dad had been in church every Sunday with his wife and daughter ever since Mom and I had started attending there when I was nine.

"Well," Pastor Adams said, "that's our group. Six boys. Three girls." He glanced to the back of the room at Mr. and Mrs. Emery, our other adult chaperones. "Think we can handle that?"

"No problem," Mr. Emery said.

"All right then." Pastor Adams tapped his knees with the palms of his hands and stood. "I'll call Hayden and tell him it's a go."

Madison looked up from her list of things to and not to bring. "Hayden?"

"Hayden Craig," Pastor Adams said. "He's going to be our guide. It's what he does for a living. He's giving us a substantial discount because he's a friend of mine, which is the only reason we can afford him. He's got two teenagers, Jacy and Dakota, who will also be coming along with us."

"Hey, a new boy to meet," Madison whispered to Rachel and me.

Rachel smiled politely but disinterestedly. I didn't even bother smiling. The way I saw it, adding a boy to the equation of my life would only further jumble things and make the answer even more difficult to come up with.

I declined several invitations from several of the youth group kids—including one from Ezra and Rachel—to go out for pizza or whatever after the meeting. It was rude and I knew it, since Mom hadn't given me a time to be home and I could have gone out socializing if I'd wanted to. I just didn't want to. I reasoned that I'd probably wind up having more than enough of these people during our hike and hurried out to my car to head back home.

But when I reached our corner, I didn't feel like turning, so I kept heading south and then drove west across the top of the rimrocks overlooking the biggest part of the city in the ancient Yellowstone River valley below.

Part of me wished that I could just keep driving forever, but the bigger part of me called myself stupid right out loud and turned the car back toward home.

At our street I could see clearly that my father's pickup was still parked in our driveway. The urge to drive by and try coming home again in an hour or so nearly overpowered me, but I pulled my car into the driveway and past my father's truck into the garage.

In the quiet darkness of my car, I did something I hadn't done in weeks . . . months, maybe.

I prayed.

I didn't know what to say to my father or what not to say.

"Help this not to turn into another fight," I whispered to God. "All I want is to get past them to my room."

The few steps from my car to the door seemed like a thousand, and it was as if I could hear sand grating against cement beneath each one.

It had taken courage for my father to come back, hadn't it?

Yes. It had.

And it was strong and gracious of Mom to accept his apology and his new confession of faith and his promised intention to try to do right by us again, wasn't it?

Yes. It was.

And it was good of God, wasn't it, to draw both of my parents to Himself after they'd made such a mess of their lives and of mine?

Yes. It was good of God to do that.

And it was good of Him to allow me to know Him too.

So if everyone was so brave and compassionate and trusting, and if God was so good, why was I so angry and confused? Was I really expected to forgive and re-embrace the man who had abandoned and hurt me just because he was my father and was a Christian now . . . or because I was a Christian now?

I thought that maybe I was supposed to . . . and that made me angry.

I managed a few civil words and even a smile for my father when I finally got inside the house, but I stayed standing behind one of the pushed-in dining room chairs and shook my head when Mom asked me if I wanted to have dessert with them.

"I was just about to serve the cake," she said. "It's German chocolate. Your favorite."

I looked at my mother. So vulnerable. So eager for me to accept her acceptance of my father. I looked at my father. So tired looking and yet strong. He looked only slightly older than the way I remembered him looking on the day he'd left. I'd kissed him goodbye before school just like I did every morning. The hug hadn't been any longer or the goodbye any more final, but when I'd come home that afternoon, Dad's stuff was gone and Mom was crying and Grandpa had put me on his lap to tell me the news.

"Daddy went away for a while, honey," he'd said.

"When's he coming back?" I'd asked. Dad had gone away several times on business, so there was nothing shocking about the news itself. Combined with Mom's behavior, though, and with Grandpa's seriousness, it had turned my mouth dry.

"I don't know, honey," he'd said.

And that had been that. At least he hadn't told me that Daddy had died and gone away forever to heaven.

I hadn't known what other questions to ask and none of the adults had volunteered any more information, only the opinion repeated by my grandfather and uncles over the years that my father was an irresponsible and selfish jerk.

It was an opinion I'd resisted at first, but had decided to embrace when I still hadn't heard from him by my thirteenth birthday.

"I'm not in the mood for cake," I told my mother now. "But thanks for making my favorite."

She nodded. "You can have a piece for breakfast."

I smiled. That would work.

"I hear you're thinking about going backpacking with the youth group," my father ventured.

I was determined to keep my face and my tone expressionless. "Yes."

"I've done quite a bit of that," he said. "If you need any equip—"

"There's an outfitter providing all the stuff," I said.

"That'll get the job done," he said.

"Sure will." I tapped the top of the chair in front of me.

"Have you got good hiking boots?" he asked me.

"Good enough," I said, even though I couldn't be sure I even owned a pair. "If not, I'll wear my running shoes."

He shook his head. "You'll want good sturdy boots that support your ankles. I can take you to pick some out if you'd like. You'll want to do it soon, so you can wear them here and there and br—"

"I'm sure the people at the shoe store can help me." I lifted my hands from the back of the chair. "Well, I guess I'll turn in. See you in the morning, Mom."

"Goodnight, Taren," Mom said.

My father said goodnight to me too, but I ignored him.

I turned my music on as soon as I'd shut my bedroom door to cover the noise of my parents' conversation downstairs.

Strange. I'd spent so many nights in my room longing to hear my parents talking downstairs again and now that they were I was deliberately drowning out the noise.

I sat on my bed and forced myself to think about the backpacking trip I'd agreed to go on. Talk about strange. I'd never been the outdoorsy-adventurer type. I liked the mountains well enough, from a distance, but they had never beckoned to me or been the stuff of my dreams. They were just dirt and rock and trees. And to go there with the church youth group? People I'd been working so diligently to avoid.

It made no sense that I'd agreed to go and that I fully intended to go through with it. What made even less sense was that I was actually excited about it.

But nothing in my life made sense anymore. Why should this be any different?

After getting into my nightshirt and moving my throw pillows to the foot of my bed, I noticed my Bible upside down on the floor underneath my nightstand. It had been months since I'd even touched it I realized, as I reached slowly for it and then returned it to its spot in the drawer.

I thought for a moment about making a note to bring it with me, but then decided that I wouldn't want the extra weight in my pack and that I'd certainly hear enough about God from Pastor Adams and probably from his outfitter friend that I wouldn't need it anyway. Still, my fingertips lingered on the cool leather cover for several seconds before I lifted them to push the drawer shut and turn out my lamp.

CHAPTER 03

"I can't believe you've lived in Billings your entire life and have never been camping in the mountains." Madison reached into her bag of trail mix for what had to be her twentieth handful in the fifteen minutes we'd been on the road. "I mean, I've never been camping either, but I'm from Chicago."

"Well, you know how it is," I said. "You pay big bucks to go see other places far away and never think about all the places in your own backyard." I nodded and helped myself to some of Madison's trail mix when she held her bag out to me. "Thanks. Besides, my mom isn't really into the great outdoors."

"Mine either," she said. "What about your dad?"

"He says he is," I said. "But I wouldn't really know. He doesn't live with us."

"Isn't that your dad who sits with you and your mom in church?" She dug into her trail mix again. "Sorry. None of my business."

I watched her eat a few more handfuls as we drove south along the narrow two-lane highway toward the mountains we could already see even though they were still more than forty miles away. "How do you eat so much and stay so thin?" I couldn't help asking her.

"That was rude," she pointed out around another mouthful of nuts, raisins, dried fruit, and stick pretzels. Then she shrugged. "I came straight from gymnastics so I'm hungry."

14

"I've always wanted to do gymnastics," I told her. "Is it as fun as it looks?"

"It can be lots of work," she said. "Especially when your mom is kind of obsessed with getting you as far as you can get in it." She laughed. "She almost wasn't going to let me come on this hike because I might hurt myself or something, but then my dad reminded her that God is more important than gymnastics and this hike is a youth group thing."

"Don't remind me," I muttered.

She squinted at me but didn't say anything.

I turned away from her and stared out the window at the drying fields along the roadside. August was always dry in this part of Montana, which was why Pastor Adams had scheduled this trip when he had.

"It won't be much fun if we get rained on every night," he'd said. "Any other month but August, and you couldn't rule snow out either."

"You can never completely rule out snow in the mountains, Dad," Ezra had pointed out.

"True enough."

The three weeks between signing up for the trip and pulling out of the parking lot in the big church van had been so stressful for me, though, that even the prospect of pitching my tent in a snowdrift couldn't have kept me home.

Mom and my father had started talking about the possibility of starting to *talk about* the possibility of trying to rebuild their marriage.

The thought of it was enough to tighten my sinuses.

Pastor Adams's cell phone played its little tune, and he picked it up. "This is Bruce," he said. This was followed by a series of *oh no's*, which was followed by an *all right, then* or two. Then Pastor Adams said, "Well, you just take care of yourself, and we'll see you when we get back." Then he snapped his phone shut and set it back in his cup holder.

"What's up?" Ezra asked him.

"Mr. Emery's hand accidentally got caught in their tailgate when Mrs. Emery was slamming it shut after loading the last of their gear this morning, and he's broken four of his fingers."

Ezra grimaced. "Ouch. That would not be good."

"The Emerys are our chaperones, aren't they?" Madison leaned forward to ask.

"They were," Pastor Adams answered. "But given the circumstances . . ."

Ezra slapped his father's back. "Looks like you're on your own, Pop. Think you can handle us?"

"We'll be wi-wee good," Payne the Pain promised. He'd exaggerated the plea in his tone so much that everyone laughed.

"I'm sure you will be," Pastor Adams said, "but Mrs. Emery found a replacement. He's going to meet us up there."

"Good," Ezra said. He glanced over his shoulder at Rachel, Madison, and me, and then looked at his father again. "Nobody for the girls' tent?"

"I'm sure Hayden's daughter will be willing to help if they need it."

"We won't need it," Madison assured him.

I wondered how she could be so sure about that since she'd already told us that she'd never been camping. But I didn't ask her. If there was one thing I'd learned about Madison Petrik during the past three weeks, it was that she was obnoxiously sure of herself, and that she usually had reason to be. She'd defeated all of the boys except Corey—Mr. Football of Billings Skyview High School—at arm wrestling one night after youth group when one of the boys had made another comment about her not being able to carry her backpack. That had led to a foot race in the parking lot the following Saturday before youth group, which Madison also won. Rizzo—Mr. My-Pocket-Computer-Game-Is-Never-Farther-Than-Six-Inches-From-My-Person of Billings Senior High School—had then suggested a video game challenge, which

Madison said she'd gladly attempt if he would agree to attempt her balance beam routine.

Nobody had made any more challenges after that, and everyone had stopped doubting Madison's ability to carry her own pack.

The way I saw it, she'd probably be able to carry mine right along with hers if it got to be too much for me.

But I had no intention of letting that happen. Especially now that there wouldn't be a woman along to offer sympathy in the event that I did feel like engaging in a little whining.

We stopped in Red Lodge to do some sightseeing. But since all of us, even Madison, had already seen Red Lodge at least in the winter during ski season, we decided we might as well head straight for the pass and get where we were going.

Pastor Adams turned off the air conditioning in the van and rolled down his window. The air cooled as we drove further into the mountains, and we breathed the fragrance of pine, fresh and full and richer than any wreath at Christmas time.

I had never been up the Beartooth Pass. I could remember one time driving a snowmobile up to where they'd put the Road Closed gate for winter, but that had been near the bottom of the switchbacks that we'd take all the way up the side of the mountain today.

Back and forth up the steep slope.

Rock wall, cemented over in some places to keep the mountain in place, rose up first on the left side of the van and sloping down on the right with only a thin guardrail between us and the ledge and lots of treetops below. Then we'd turn a corner and the ledge would be on our left. Back. Forth. Back. Forth. Up. Up. Up.

My hands loosened their hold on the edge of my seat during the sections of the switchbacks when the slope down was to the left of us. Somehow, even though the newly placed state-of-the-art guardrails still looked incredibly flimsy, there was at least the perception of added security with the other lane of highway between us and the ledge.

Frightening though the trek up was, it was worth it on account of the views of the valley below and of the small pockets of perfectly clear blue water that dotted many of the jagged rock peaks and plateaus.

And, of course, there was snow.

Pastor Adams had planned to let us out at a spot near the summit to play in it, but several tourists with license plates from places like Texas and Louisiana and Arizona on their way either into or out of Yellowstone Park were already there. They had pulled off the road to record their children sledding down one of the small slopes on black garbage sacks or on their jackets. We decided not to stop and further hog the snow since we all saw more than enough of it each winter. And besides, it was cold outside. We kept driving.

"This is the most awesome road," Madison said once we'd descended from the summit past all the fields of rocks, grass, pools of water, and wildflowers and finally back into the trees again heading down the other side of the mountain to Cooke Pass.

"Sure is," I agreed.

"Will we get up as high as the snow on our hike?" she asked Pastor Adams.

"We'll get above the tree line," he said, "and we'll camp at a couple of lakes that sometimes keep snow at the edges all year long. But except for the glacier, we shouldn't be hiking through any snow, no."

"Good," she said. "Because it was cold up there."

"It'll be cold at night," Ezra told her. "But Mr. Craig's got sleeping bags that'll keep you warm down to forty below outside."

"It's not going to be that cold, is it?"

Pastor Adams laughed. "No. It can get down to the twenties though. Above zero, I mean."

Madison grimaced and looked at me. "And we're doing this because . . . ?"

"Uh . . . because it's going to be fun?"

"Exactly," Ezra said.

I smiled even as I shook my head. Clearly, Ezra Adams had learned somewhere along the line to take that "if there be any praise, think on these things" scripture to extremes.

But even if *fun* didn't turn out to be my adjective of choice for this hike, it would definitely be *fine* to be away from home and from Mom and most of all from my father.

CHAPTER 04

If I had taken the time to formulate a mental picture of what a mountain outfitter might look like, I was sure it would have been very similar to the appearance of the man who stepped out onto his deck when Pastor Adams stopped the church van in the dirt driveway, except that Hayden Craig didn't have a beard, didn't have a wad of chewing tobacco in his cheek, and wasn't wearing a baseball cap. He did, however, have on hiking boots, tan jeans, a thick flannel shirt jacket—a deep teal shade, though, instead of the traditional chunky plaid I would have predicted—and one of those thick three-buckle leather watchbands. He was tall and rugged looking, and I knew right off that I wasn't going to want to get on his bad side.

"He looks like a guy I saw trying to sell swords on one of those shopping channels," Madison whispered to me.

I nodded. That was exactly what he looked like. Or more precisely maybe, it was just the overall demeanor that was the same. That don't-mess-with-me set to the jaw and eyes.

Of course Mr. Craig would want to establish his authority right away. Especially with a group of teenagers. City teenagers at that.

I watched Pastor Adams approach him, and I watched the two men embrace. This was definitely something I would not have suspected the stern-featured Hayden Craig capable of, and I decided that I'd better not prejudge him based on some knife salesman stereotype.

Still, I hastily rolled my hair into a bun at the back of my head and then slid my ponytail holder off my wrist to twist around it. I didn't want Mr. Craig to think I was the typical swishy-haired city girl who'd be completely inept in the mountains . . . even though that's probably exactly what I was.

I didn't want his son to think that either. Dakota Craig was a very attractive guy. My age I figured. Strong and capable looking like his father, with the same gray eyes.

"Glad to have you," he said after Ezra had introduced him and his older sister Jacy to all of us. Then he glanced over at our van. "Weren't you bringing a couple more adults?" he asked Ezra.

"We've got one more coming." Ezra grinned at Jacy. "But our girls are kind of on their own here." He explained to her about Mr. and Mrs. Emery. Then he smiled at her again. "You are planning on hiking with us, aren't you?"

She smiled back. "Wouldn't miss it."

Clearly these two had met before, and clearly the experience had been positive.

"Come on, girls," Jacy said to Rachel, Madison, and me. "Let's go get our gear set up before the guys come inside and hog the best of it." She smiled at Ezra again and then led us up the steps past her father and inside the house.

If I had taken the time to formulate a mental picture of what the inside of a mountain outfitter's cabin might look like, it would have been nothing like what I saw as I followed Jacy through the front room, past the dining room, and into the supply room at the back of the back hallway. There were the mandatory deer and elk racks hung here and there on the thick log walls, as well as two or three genuine bear rugs on the wood plank floors. But that was where my preconceived ideas had to defer to reality.

The furnishings were rustic looking, but tastefully so, and they were not old or thick with the smell of hunters who'd spent way too many days in the forest with no baths and with frozen and thawed elk "scent" permeating their clothing. Even though the main part of the cabin was obviously several decades old, its decor had been updated recently enough to accommodate a color scheme of muted blues, deep greens, burgundies, and tans. There was nothing fancy or pretentious about the place, and neither had it been neglected to create some falsely rugged backwoodsy image.

It was a house in the mountains. Nothing more. Nothing less. A house, I noticed later, with a spectacular river rock fireplace.

"Did your dad do that by hand?" I asked Jacy late in the afternoon when we girls were sitting in front of the fire she had built.

"Yup," she said.

"It's gorgeous," Rachel said.

"Yup," Jacy said again.

"Do you like living way up here and so by yourselves?" Madison asked her.

I glanced from Madison back to Jacy and waited for her answer. The town of Cooke Pass, which really was nothing more than a cluster of cabins in a meadow just off one side of the highway and a café on the other, had just kind of appeared in the middle of so much vast wilderness and seemed to disappear just as quickly. The Craigs' cabin was not in the main group of cabins, but was a couple miles further up the highway and back another half-mile or so on an uphill dirt road into thick trees. So Jacy and her brother and father really didn't even live in the little town that really couldn't even be called a town. And I knew that the Beartooth Pass was closed during the winter, so that would make getting out of Cooke Pass to anywhere civilized an even longer excursion. Probably all the way through Yellowstone Park.

But again, and firmly, Jacy's answer was, "Yup. Only we're not by ourselves so much anymore. The business is doing really well, and it seems like we've almost always got someone scheduled for something."

"All year long?" Madison asked.

22

"Yup. We get a few off weeks. This year we went to Florida and it was a lot of fun."

"Wow," Madison said. "I bet that was a change for you."

"Oh yeah." Jacy smiled. "We went in February, so it wasn't too hot there, and we got a week away from hauling firewood and getting up at two in the morning to throw more logs in the wood-stove and shoveling off the roof and needing fifteen minutes prep-time before walking out the front door just to pile on your winter gear. Plus it was a week off of homeschooling." She stared at the fire for a few seconds. "But I was glad to get back to my own room and back on the snowmobile trails."

"What did your dad think of Florida?" Rachel wanted to know.

"He used to be an accountant in Milwaukee, so he was actually more used to big city things than Dakota and me." She smiled. "He had a great time, but he was glad to get home too."

Madison leaned forward in her overstuffed chair and rested her elbows on her knees. "So tell me how an accountant from Milwaukee ends up leading wilderness adventures out of this tiny little Montana place."

"It's kind of a long story," Jacy said, and I thought I saw a flicker of hurt in the way she diverted her eyes from Madison's just for a second before adding, "and it's his place to tell it, not mine."

"I was just curious," Madison said, visibly surprised by Jacy's tactful yet definitive version of mind-your-own-business.

"You'll find that my dad is a very private person," Jacy said. "He likes to keep a professional distance between us and our clients." She shrugged. "I'm sure you can understand that."

"Sure," Madison said.

Jacy smiled. "Every now and then though, if he decides a person is decent enough, he'll open up a little." She laughed. "You may still think he's rude after this hike, but I can guarantee you he's much better about it than he was even a year ago. And a lot of that has to do with your pastor."

"Pastor Adams?" Rachel asked.

"Yeah. His wife died too, and—"

"I'm sorry," Rachel said, "about your mom. Ezra told us."

"Thanks." Jacy nodded. "Anyway, Pastor Adams has helped Dad a lot. He's still being stubborn about becoming a Christian, though, even though Dakota and me have both done it. That's one of the reasons I've been so excited about you guys coming." She leaned forward and added another log to her fire. "A whole week for my dad with nobody but Christians."

Poor guy was my initial thought until it occurred to me that Jacy was apparently hoping and expecting that we'd be able to minister to her father.

If only she knew how far away from being able to minister to anybody I was. During the past few months, I hadn't even been able to keep my own faith strong. In fact, the greater part of me hadn't even attempted or wanted to try, because what I'd really wanted when I'd first seen my father again was to be angry.

Of course Jacy had no way of knowing any of that. She probably thought we'd all be great and victorious Christians as she knew Ezra and his dad to be. And she'd probably been praying for weeks that one of us would have the words to penetrate her father's soul. Words that she herself had not yet stumbled upon.

The realization that someone was actually expecting something out of my supposed Christianity made me cold suddenly, even though I was right beside Jacy's very steady and very warm fire.

"Well anyway," I said as I zipped my jacket up a little more snugly against my chin, "we can pray for him."

I had used those words as an escape, as a cop-out, really, but Jacy eagerly accepted them as much more than that. "Thank you," she said.

"So," I said because it was past time to change the subject, "who do you suppose the Emerys recruited to come in their place?"

"One of the other youth staff, I'm sure," Rachel said. "Maybe even Pastor Kent."

"No," Madison said. "He's going to be preaching Sunday."

"Well whoever it is," Jacy said, "he's in for a treat. The trail is perfect this year. Not too much water on account of it hasn't been raining much. That means fewer bugs, easier walking, and great fishing." She stood and adjusted the logs in the fire once more and then returned the poker to its stand. "The only bad thing about a dry year is that the rockslide sections of the trail are a little dustier and more slippery."

"Rockslides?" Madison asked. "Sounds dangerous."

"No, they're just bare slopes where old rockslides have taken out all the trees and now there's just dirt and rock all the way up and down the mountain," Jacy assured us. "The trail itself is just as wide and just as good there as it is anywhere else, except in one spot where it's been washed out completely and you just sort of have to make your way up this rock chute. But it's doable. And it's great scenery." She paused. "Kind of eerie at certain times of the day because of the sunlight and because of it being so big and empty."

I couldn't picture what she was talking about, but figured I'd find out in person soon enough.

"I hear a vehicle coming," Jacy said. "I guess you're about to find out who your mystery chaperone is."

I couldn't hear any vehicle, but I followed Jacy and the other girls out onto the front deck. Sure enough, there were reflective flashes in the trees and in a matter of moments I began to hear the hum of an engine and the sound of tires on small rocks and dirt.

Mr. Craig and Pastor Adams walked down the steps and waited at the bottom for the vehicle to emerge from the trees into the parking area.

As soon as the all-too-familiar silver pickup pulled into view, I felt my stomach tighten until it seemed it would explode. I tried to inhale and to swallow, but all that would work were my legs as I stumbled quietly to the nearest bench and sat heavily on it.

The truck stopped, the driver's side door opened, and my father stepped out to greet Pastor Adams and Mr. Craig. He looked for me, saw me, held my eyes with his for a moment, and then distractedly turned his attention back to the two men who were asking him about his drive up.

Jacy sat down beside me. "Are you okay, Taren? You don't look good all of a sudden."

All I could manage was a shrug.

"Could be the altitude," she said. "That happens. You need to drink lots of water." She took gentle hold of my arm, helped me to stand up, and then led me back inside. "Sit by the fire. I'll bring you some."

"Thanks."

But I knew good and well that water was not what I needed.

I needed to scream.

No. I needed to get a grip on my emotions and, more importantly, figure out a way to get myself out of this hike.

An hour later after I'd called home and left a message on Mom's answering machine for her to call me as soon as she got home, and after Jacy and Dakota had taken everyone but Pastor Adams, their father, and me into Cooke City for dinner, I sat alone on the front deck watching evening take hold of the forest around me. My stomach had loosened up once I'd gotten permission to call Mom, and even more when my father had agreed to go to dinner at Pastor Adams' prompting.

"I'll go back to Billings," I'd overheard my father saying to Pastor Adams. "It was my first thought to say 'no way' when Sue called me, but then I thought . . . maybe . . ."

"We need you along, Will," Pastor Adams had insisted. "The kids' permission slips state that there'll be at least two chaperones from our church, and I know you're very competent out here. Probably more competent than anyone else who could have come. This is something Taren is going to have to make the decision about."

Well I'd made my decision. I was going to go home.

As I sat on first the bench and then moved to one of the steps, I wondered where my mom could be. Then I wondered if she knew that Dad had come up to chaperone us. Then I wondered if she'd put him up to it.

Then my stomach tightened up again.

"Feeling any better?"

I turned at the man's voice behind me just as the screen door closed behind him. "No."

"It's too bad," Mr. Craig said. He sat on the bench where I'd been sitting. "It's a once-in-a-lifetime experience, this hike."

"Yeah, well . . ."

"You'll probably feel better in the morning," he said. "Once you get a good night's sleep and get acclimated to the altitu—"

"It's not the altitude, Mr. Craig," I said in frustration. "It's . . ." I stood, climbed the steps back up to the deck, and sat on the bench across from his with my back to the railing.

Hadn't Jacy said he was a private person? He'd guard what I told him, wouldn't he, if I told him the truth? Then he'd understand and wouldn't think I was just wimping out on the hike. "You know Will, the other guy who is going to chaperone us?" I waited for him to acknowledge me with a nod. "He's my father."

Hayden Craig stared at me. Then he grinned. "And what? He won't let you date the loser you've got a crush on so you're ticked at him?"

"Okay . . . see . . ." Hadn't Jacy also mentioned that we might think her father was rude? Yes, she had. And she had been right. So now, even though nothing about my father and me was any of this man's business, my anger fueled my mouth before reason could remind me to take a moment to consider whether I really wanted to elaborate. "No," I said coldly. "He packed up and left Mom and me when I was seven. We never saw him again until six months ago when he shows up on our doorstep saying he's changed, he's a Christian now, he's sorry, and all of a sudden he wants to do right by us. My mother is falling all over herself to believe him, but I'm kind of having some trouble with it and the only reason I came on this hike was to get away from him and now he's here and . . ."

I was rambling like an idiot. Letting words tumble out of my mouth on the strength and ugliness of emotions that I'd tried to contain inside for months. While some guidance counselor might think it constructive for me to vent my true feelings aloud, I wasn't so sure that Mr. Hayden Craig was an appropriate—or interested—audience. "I'm sorry," I told him. "I . . . I'm sorry."

He stayed quiet for several minutes, not looking away from me. Finally, he said, "I'm sorry too. That's rough about your dad."

"So you understand why I want to go home?" I asked, somewhat surprised by the fact that his understanding even mattered to me.

"Yeah, I understand," he said. "But can I tell you something?"

"Sure." He'd listened to me. The least I could do was hear him out in return. Besides, given what Jacy had said about his keeping that professional distance, I felt somewhat honored that he was even talking with me. Could it be that I had somehow stumbled into the category of the decent enough few that he'd open up to?

No. It was much more likely that I'd simply made enough of a fool of myself that he couldn't resist his duty as an adult to tell me how stupid I was being.

Either way, I owed it to him to listen to what he had to say.

He took in a long breath and then let it out slowly through tight lips. "When my wife died," he said quietly, "her family blamed me. We'd been on vacation up here, and she'd gotten very sick. They figured that if we'd been home in Milwaukee, she'd have had better medical care, and she wouldn't have died of a simple flu. They figured that if I'd been a decent and caring and responsible husband, I'd have taken her to Billings right away." He looked away from me then, beyond me to the trees. "I thought she had the flu, you know? I mean, she *did* have the flu . . ."

"Mr. Craig," I said, seeing his evident discomfort with this memory and regretting having given him reason to revisit it, "you don't have to—"

He held up his hand but still didn't look back at me. "My point is this: They've never forgiven me. And I think most people would think that their rejection of me and the kids is wrong."

"Sure it is," I said.

Now he looked straight at me. "So if they ever showed up here, on my doorstep, telling me they've had a change of heart, they're sorry they blamed me, and asked me to forgive them . . ."

I leaned forward, fully expecting him to say that he'd never even consider it, and that not only that, he'd have them off his property faster than a lightning strike.

"I guess I'd be grateful for that day," he said.

"Well." I was stunned. "Your situation is different," I said defensively. "In their minds, you did something wrong, and that's why they did what they did. I never did anything to my dad, and he still took off."

"I'm sure it had nothing to do with you," he agreed.

"So it's different," I insisted.

"Yeah. It's different. Still, I'll never have the opportunity you have, I'm sure of it, to see things right between people who should . . . be there for each other."

I shook my head. "So you're telling me you'd just fall at their feet with tears in your eyes and say, 'Yes, oh yes, I forgive you'?"

He laughed. A long tension-filled laugh. "No. I'm not telling you that. It would be difficult, but it would honor my wife. It would be good for me, for them, and most importantly it would be good for my kids to be able to have a relationship with their grandparents again." He shrugged. "And it would just plain be the right thing to do."

"Now you sound like my mother and like Pastor Adams and like everyone else I know," I muttered.

He leaned back against his house and folded his arms across his chest.

He didn't need to say a word and he knew it.

I stood up, shoved my hands into my pockets, and took his steps two at a time down to the dirt parking area. A walk in the trees suddenly sounded very appealing. Before I left though, I turned back to the man on the deck. "I'm sorry your wife's family treated you that way. It could only have made everything harder."

He nodded. "I'm sorry about the way you were treated too."

I smiled. Whether he agreed with my decision to leave or not, I felt certain that he at least understood it. I waved to him and turned away.

"There are bears in the woods," he said behind me.

I spun around to face him again. "Bears?"

"Yeah. You know, those big brown or black things with nasty-smelling teeth and long deadly claws?"

I laughed. "I know what a bear is. Are they really around here?"

"I wouldn't say they were if they weren't," he said.

"Well, then," I said, climbing the steps back to the deck and sitting on the bench across from him again, "maybe I'll just hang out here. I don't want to miss my mom's call, anyway."

"Good idea."

I turned on the bench to lean my elbows on the railing and my chin on my arms. The quiet of the place amazed me. There was no sound except an occasional bird, a few flying insects, and the touches of the slight breeze in the tops of the trees.

"It really does sound like whispering," I said aloud.

"Sorry?"

"The wind," I explained to Mr. Craig. "You always read things about the whispering wind. I always thought that was kind of stupid, but it really does sound like that."

Pastor Adams joined Mr. Craig and me on the deck then, and the three of us sat, mostly in silence, for nearly an hour before the telephone rang inside the house.

As Mr. Craig stood stiffly and made his way inside to answer it, I prepared to get up and follow him. I felt sure it was my mother calling.

The trouble was that I was no longer so sure about what I wanted to tell her. Mr. Craig's comments had made some sense to me and had calmed me. So had the peacefulness of the place. It might be good for my father and me to have some time together up here and away from Mom. I might be able to get to re-know him without the constant fear whenever I saw him and Mom together that they'd be sitting me down to discuss—no, announce— the inevitability and rightness of their remarriage. Maybe we'd have the opportunity to bond over conquering a giant stone rockface together or something movie-ish like that.

Or maybe we'd just get on each other's nerves and neither of us would enjoy the hike.

Either way, I decided as I stood at Mr. Craig's call and walked inside the house to take the phone from him, I didn't want to wimp out and run from this situation anymore. The way I perceived things, that's what my father had done for whatever reason, when he'd left Mom and me. How could I justify being angry with him for doing it to me and then turn around and do the exact same thing in response?

I couldn't.

"Thank you," I said to Mr. Craig.

He left quickly, but I wouldn't have minded if he'd stayed. In fact, I might have actually preferred it. He could have given me moral support. A thumb's-up or something.

I spoke with my mother for a couple minutes and found out that she did indeed know that my father had come up here, but only because she'd just heard his message telling her so right before she'd heard mine. She asked me if I was still feeling sick and said she'd understand if I wanted to come home even if I wasn't.

"Mom," I interrupted her to say, "it's okay now, and . . . I think I'm going to go ahead and stay."

Once I said goodbye to my mother and hung up the phone, I knew I had to stick to my decision. My own stubbornness, if nothing else, would forbid my changing my mind no matter how badly I might want to.

For once in my life my stubbornness might turn out to be a good thing, I mused five minutes later when Dakota and Jacy returned with our crew of hikers . . . and with my father.

CHAPTER **06**

"Does that feel right?"

I smiled at Jacy, who'd just adjusted my shoulder straps after helping me get into my loaded backpack for the first time. "I might be able to answer that question," I said, "except that I really couldn't tell you how it's supposed to feel, so I wouldn't know if it felt right or not."

Jacy laughed. Then she was all business. She had other hikers to tend to. "It's supposed to feel like the weight is on your hips and not on your shoulders," she said.

I paid as much attention as I knew how to to the dispersion of the twenty-nine or so pounds on my back and still couldn't answer Jacy's question except to say that my pack didn't feel as heavy as I'd thought it would when I'd lifted it up to get into it.

"That's what you want," she said. "Just that all the weight isn't hanging off your shoulders." Then she moved on to assist Rachel, leaving me to stare in somewhat stupefied disbelief at the mountain this pack on my back and I were about to attempt to conquer.

Well, *conquer* might be too strong of a word, I admitted to myself. Actually, now that I really had the pack on my back and there was no getting out of this hike, I wondered if the word *survive* might even be stretching the boundaries of what I could reasonably hope to accomplish.

"All set?" Mr. Craig asked me as he passed by me. His pack looked huge compared to mine, but he didn't even seem to notice its weight.

I thought of the trail ahead. Twenty-something miles. The twenty-nine pounds on my back. Bears. My father. "Sure," I said to Mr. Craig, smiling as I did. "No problem."

He stopped walking and turned to look right at me. "I'll be looking after you," he said. Then he approached the trailhead. "I need everyone to listen to me."

Everyone stopped what they were doing and gave him their full attention.

Mr. Craig pointed at Pastor Adams and then at my father. "You two lead out this morning," he said. "Dakota and Jacy, you find places in the middle of the group. And I'll pull up the back."

It was evident in the confused expressions on Jacy and Dakota's faces that this was a departure from how their father normally did things, but neither of them questioned him.

"We'll take a break after half an hour or so to see how everyone's doing," he continued. "In all, we're going to get in three miles today." He directed his next comment to our group of boys. "Pace yourselves in the uphill."

Madison raised her hand.

Mr. Craig acknowledged her with a nod.

"Are there snakes or lions or bears or anything around?"

"Oh my," Payne Chisholm sang out and the whole group of boys, except Ezra and Dakota, laughed.

Mr. Craig ignored them. "Not many mountain lions, Madison," he said. "No snakes. But coyotes, yes. Wolves, potentially. And bears, yes. Each of the adults has a canister of concentrated pepper spray in case we encounter anything unfriendly, and I've got my handgun. Just be sure to stay in sight of either Pastor Adams, Will, Jacy, Dakota, or me and everything'll be fine."

He scanned the group. "Any more questions?"

"What if someone gets hurt, or something?"

This came from Madison again, and it surprised me. She was usually so confident and unshakable. Now she sounded almost frightened.

Truth be told, though, we were probably all frightened to one degree or another. It was just that Madison was the only one bold enough to not try to hide it.

"I'll take care of them," Mr. Craig assured her. "But I get paid to make as sure as a person can that that doesn't happen."

"And he's good at what he does," Jacy said.

"The best," added Pastor Adams.

"But what if *you* get hurt?" Madison pressed.

Mr. Craig squinted at her, making me suspect that the possibility may honestly have never occurred to him.

"Well," he said, "then we'll punt. But Jacy and Dakota, along with your pastor, did finish a hike without me last year after I came down with pneumonia midway through."

Madison's hold on her shoulder straps seemed to loosen a bit as she looked at Jacy. "That must have been scary."

Jacy nodded.

"And just so you know," Pastor Adams said, "Will, here, did quite a bit of mountain guiding in Alaska." He slapped my father's arm with the back of his hand. "Including some high mountain rescue with the Alaska National—"

"Well, there you have it," Mr. Craig said to Madison. "I'd say you're in all kinds of capable hands."

"Not to mention God's," Jacy said, earning a disapproving glance from her father.

After that, Madison didn't venture any more questions and nobody else did either.

Mr. Craig stood at the trailhead as first Pastor Adams, then my father, then Ezra, then our five other boys, then Jacy, then Dakota, then Madison, and then me and Rachel passed by him. Then he followed the group of us onto the trail.

Fourteen in all.

I wanted to thank Mr. Craig for seeing to it that I had a choice whether or not to walk near my father, but I wasn't completely sure that that had been his intention by assigning my father to the lead. Still, whether it had been his intention or just the result of his wanting to walk at the back of the pack for a change, I was grateful to him.

I said nothing though, because Rachel was between me and Mr. Craig and she'd already started talking to him.

About God.

"I knew when I was eight years old that I was going to be a missionary," she was telling him.

I felt sorry for the man. At least three of the youth in our group, not to mention Pastor Adams, were very outspoken Christians, most notably Rachel. And since Jacy had let it be known that her father had not yet accepted Christ . . . well, Rachel would want to be trying to do something about that.

"Oh yeah?" Mr. Craig replied behind her. His tone was more disinterested than irritated.

Rachel seemed to take that as encouragement to continue. "Yes, sir. See . . ."

I paid attention to the trail. To the rhythmic sound of my boots against the hard-packed earth. To the sounds of things settling in my backpack. To the squeaky sound of my sleeping bag rubbing against the top bar of my pack frame. To the scent of pine. To Madison, who was getting further ahead of me.

But when Rachel said, "When my real father died when I was eight," I started paying attention to her again.

When her real father had died? That would mean that Mr. Moore, the man who was always in church with Rachel and her mother, had to be her stepfather. And it would also mean that Rachel wasn't as strong as she was in her faith because her life had been perfect. In fact, she and I had apparently been right around the same age when our fathers had disappeared from our lives. Only Rachel had never had the hope of being able to see hers again. Not until heaven anyway. I'd at least had hope, even if it had turned out to be in vain.

Of course, all my hoping hadn't turned out to be completely in vain, had it? At this moment, less than a half-mile separated my father and me, and I could march up the trail and hike right beside him at any moment I chose.

Not so for Rachel Moore.

"I remember going to my knees to say my prayers before bed the night of his accident," Rachel was saying, "and thanking God that I knew my daddy was in heaven with Him, and it was like a real voice came into my head and told me that it was my job to help other people not to be sad when someone they loved died because they could know for sure that they'd gone to heaven."

Even though Rachel gave him several moments to respond to what she'd said, Mr. Craig said nothing.

"So that's what I'm going to do," she said finally. Quietly. Almost timidly. As if Mr. Craig's silence suddenly troubled her.

What troubled me was that she'd been so insensitive, babbling on about people dying the same as one of the boys would babble on about football when she knew good and well that Mr. Craig had lost his wife.

Of course Rachel had lost her father. Maybe that gave her a right to babble on about people dying. Death was, after all, part of life. And both she and Mr. Craig had acutely experienced losing someone to it.

"I'm sorry, Mr. Craig," Rachel said after a long time walking. "I'm thinking maybe I shouldn't have been talking about that."

"We all deal with death in our own way," he said coldly. "You got your calling from God, and I got mad at Him."

"I don't mean to keep on the point, sir," Rachel said, "but of the two responses, I'd feel a whole lot safer about mine."

Mr. Craig laughed. A genuine and relieved laugh. "Do I strike you as a person who's looking for the safest way to do things?"

"No, sir," Rachel said, laughing too. But her laugh sounded more nervous than amused.

"Just so you know," Mr. Craig said, "and so you don't lose any sleep being afraid for me, I'm not mad at God anymore."

"That's good, sir," Rachel said.

"So where are you planning to do your missionary work?" Mr. Craig asked her.

"Eastern Europe."

"Oh," he said, "they have hundred-pound trout in some of those rivers over there. Now look around you here."

Rachel stayed quiet while she did.

I lifted my eyes from the dirt just ahead of each next step and looked around too, perceiving for the first time the difference in the forest around me. Instead of dense and tall pine trees, we were walking through what had obviously been a burn area once upon a time. As far as I could see on the fields and hills on both sides of the trail, the ground was covered with white sticks. Some of them lying, some of them poking eerily toward the sky. Beneath and all around them, thick green grass grew. Grass speckled with the colors of the wildflowers that spread out in patches all throughout it. Beyond all this green and white and wildflowers, granite peaks and plateaus climbed up and encircled the valley.

"This is what I like about up here," Mr. Craig said. "It's simple. Things live. Things die. New things live."

"Simple," Rachel said, "when you're talking about trees and grass. And even hundred-pound trout. But here, and in Eastern Europe, people are dying spiritually without—"

This seemed like the perfect cue for me to start paying attention to the trail again and maybe even think about pushing my pace a bit to catch up with Madison.

The conversation behind me was a bit tense for my taste and struck me as somewhat manipulative. On both sides. Like a deliberate debate rather than simple chitchat. But I felt confident that Madison and I could busy our minds quite adequately by discussing the scenery itself or by jokingly moaning and groaning about our growing awareness of the weight on our backs.

CHAPTER 07

When we stepped onto the trail again after our first break, I decided to walk behind Dakota Craig. I wanted to find out more about him. What grade he'd be in come September. What his favorite sport was. What his favorite television show was. But come to think of it, I hadn't seen a television at the Craigs' house, so maybe Dakota didn't have a favorite show. I wanted to find out what he thought about things like gun control, capital punishment, and welfare. I wondered how a person raised in such a remote place so far away from any practical need to concern himself with these big social issues and who didn't even have a television to inform, persuade, or corrupt his thinking would develop his opinions. I suspected that Dakota's stands on the issues would reflect his father's, which I suspected would fall far to the right of any supposed political center, though not so far as to be wandering the woods in an aluminum foil hat to reflect back the government's satellite-to-human-brain propaganda.

During the half-mile or so through the thick trees and rocks before the trail started heading a bit more decisively uphill though, I concluded that Dakota was an even more private person than his father. Either that or he was shy. Or just plain rude. Most of my attempts at conversation had led absolutely nowhere, except when I'd abandoned the current events issues of the day and had asked him instead about the lake we were hiking into for this first night.

"Why is it called Lady of the Lake?" I'd asked him. "Is there some tragic story about a lost woman or something?"

He'd laughed. "Look at the map."

That had been no help, and so once the trail started heading uphill, I didn't have the breath or desire to ask him any more questions.

"You doing okay?" he asked me when we'd gone another half-mile that had felt more like a hundred.

"Yeah," I lied.

"It takes a little while to get used to the uphill," he said. He wasn't even winded.

"Uh-huh." I'd never get used to it. I felt certain I'd die first.

"We can stop for a minute if you'd like," he said. "Dad, Madison, and Rachel are still quite a ways behind us. I haven't heard them for a while."

I nodded as I sat heavily on the nearest boulder and started to wriggle free of my pack.

"Leave it on," Dakota said as he sat beside me. Then he smiled. "If you pick a sloped rock, you can use the high part of the rock to lift the weight off your back without actually taking it off. That way you won't have to pick it up to get back into it."

"Oh. Okay."

Whatever.

After I'd sipped a bit of my water and had stopped seeing bright blue spots, I thanked Dakota for letting me take a break.

"I'd rather sit now than do CPR later," he said.

"Very funny." I smiled. "So you keep your ears open for the other people on the trail?"

"Always," he said.

"Is that why you don't talk much while we're walking?"

He nodded.

"And here I was getting all offended," I teased.

"Don't do that," he said. "I liked what you had to say." He untwisted the cap off his canteen and took a couple swallows of water. "Except for the thing about feeling sorry for me because we don't have a television. When would I watch it?" He looked all around him at the trees and at the peaks we could see through the tops of them. "And who'd want to when they could be out here?"

"Lots of people," I assured him.

He looked thoughtfully at me. "Are you one of them?"

"Not yet," I told him. "But give me some rain, a bear or two, some blisters on my feet, or a forest fire, and then I might be."

"Hear that?" he asked me.

I was instantly alert. Listening.

"This first bit of the trail is a four-wheel-drive road," he said.

"This is a road?" I couldn't imagine a vehicle crawling its way over and among all the ruts and boulders we'd been stepping over and around for the past hour. But then, sure enough, I heard the whining hum of an engine, the creaking of metal against metal, the thunk of what had most likely been an axle or something smacking into a boulder.

And then I saw it. A very old, loved, and used-almost-to-the-point-of-destruction jeep. Nearly all the paint had been scratched off, and the thing had wood two-by-fours for bumpers!

I laughed aloud.

"That's Ezekiel Crenshaw," Dakota told me. "He's one of the oldest old-timers up here." He stood and raised his hand as he approached the slow-moving jeep.

Ezekiel Crenshaw looked as old and abused as his vehicle. He offered a nearly toothless grin in my direction and then winked at Dakota. "Your father's hikers keep getting prettier and prettier, Dakoty," he said.

Dakota glanced over his shoulder at me and then looked back to the old man. "Going fishing?"

"Yep."

"It looks like more trouble to drive in than it is to walk."

"I like drivin'," said Ezekiel Crenshaw. "It don't get me the whole way in, but when you're an old gizzard like me, every little bit I can save my knees helps."

Dakota stepped back from the jeep. "Well, good fishing."

Ezekiel Crenshaw nodded and eased his jeep, grinding gears, whining engine, foul-smelling blue smoke and all, forward along the trail again.

"I can't believe that thing actually runs," I said to Dakota when he sat beside me again.

He nodded. "It'll be an area legend one of these days."

Madison caught up with us then, breathlessly called us wimps, and kept walking.

"She's really something," Dakota said, watching her until she turned around a corner and disappeared behind the trees.

Was that a fond *She's really something* or a put-out one? I couldn't tell.

And at that particular moment I was too tired to care.

Dakota and I sat and rested until his father and Rachel joined us. Rachel sat down right away, but Mr. Craig didn't even stop walking. "You take the back for a while," he muttered to Dakota.

Dakota nodded at the back of his father's pack and then turned to Rachel. "He's used to a quicker pace," he said.

"I'm sure," she said.

Even though I didn't have to relift my pack to get it on my back again, its weight nearly prevented my being able to stand up. But I managed it, grabbed the bottom of the frame to reposition the monster, and then grinned with false determination at Dakota and Rachel. "I'm ready to go again."

"All right," Dakota said. "We'll be behind you in a while."

For the first time since we'd set out, I found myself completely alone on the trail. I listened and could hear Dakota and Rachel talking, and I thought I could hear Mr. Craig's pack squeaking rhythmically up ahead. But I couldn't see anyone. For the next several yards I pushed my pace. The trees on either side of me seemed to press more densely against me as the sound of my own footsteps on the earth completely filled my ears.

A bear could charge through the trees right now and claw my head off before I had a chance to open my mouth and scream and nobody would know it. And if the bear dragged me off to his favorite private dining place, Dakota and Rachel wouldn't even know I was missing until they arrived at Lady of the Lake and didn't find me there.

Even the huge sky seemed to be closer to me as I grabbed hold of my shoulder straps and gulped in enough air to support the near run I'd worked myself into.

At last, I saw the red of the sleeping bag strapped to the top of Mr. Craig's pack. I slowed my pace and shouted ahead for him to hold up.

He did. But he didn't turn around to greet me. He started walking again as soon as I'd gotten to within a couple yards of him. "What?" he said. "You going to preach at me too now?"

I didn't have the breath to preach at anyone. Especially not at his vigorous pace. And especially not to someone with an attitude as hostile as his obviously was. "Nope," I told him. "Not me."

"Hm," he muttered. "So you don't care that I'm going to hell?"

I did not appreciate the sarcasm in his tone. And I appreciated even less the prodding of my own conscience to ignore his tone and consider his question.

Did I care that as of this moment the man in front of me had not accepted Christ as Savior? Did I care that if he entered eternity before he did, he would, as Rachel had apparently been telling him to the point of his great irritation, spend it in the bad place? Without God and without hope and without end?

Did I care?

Of course I did, I guessed, but . . .

"Hey," I said, exasperated both with him and with myself, "if you don't care, why should I? I've got problems of my own."

"Fair enough," he said, and we kept walking.

Without speaking.

I thought that I should tell Mr. Craig that I did care about his soul when I really stopped and thought about it. But when I really stopped and thought about it, even that assertion would be faulty. It was an assertion made out of a spiritual knowledge about what it meant to be lost and about the torments of hell. But not an assertion based on any real burden I carried. Nothing that kept me up nights.

I went to school every day with all kinds of kids who hadn't accepted Christ, and I knew good and well that I concerned myself more with things like their clothes, their popularity, their athletic ability, their academic ability, their looks, and their opinions of me than I concerned myself with their lostness . . . or than with the fact that I could and should tell them about Jesus.

Especially more recently.

Oh, there had been times after a particularly poignant youth rally or a great youth camp experience that I'd gone back to school determined to win someone to Christ. There had been times that I'd watched people in the halls and actually felt grief for them because they didn't know the Savior who would not only rescue them from an eternity in hell but would make their here-and-now-and-until-they-died lives on earth so much more meaningful.

But times like that, moments of true compassion like that, had been few and short-lived for me. And they'd been nonexistent since my father had come back.

For a grueling half-hour I struggled inside with feeling ashamed that I didn't care more. But then I fought back and attempted to console myself with the supposition that all teenagers were basically self-absorbed, and that it was the rare teen like Ezra or Rachel who could actually see beyond who'd invite them to sit at their lunch table.

No go, though.

The fact that I was within a yard of the man in front of me and had been unable to instantly assure him—in a conversation he'd initiated—that I did want him to come to know Christ because I did care not only about his eternity but about his life now . . . It turned my hands cold even though I was sweating from my exertion on the trail.

I had no idea what to do about it. I felt as if God and the things that were important to Him were as far away from me now as was the end of this trail on the other side of these immense and daunting mountains. Maybe even farther away.

After a while Mr. Craig and I caught up to Madison and Jacy. Mr. Craig ruffled his daughter's hair but passed by her without much chitchat.

I thought about slowing my pace and staying with the girls, but they were in the middle of a giggly conversation about the boys ahead of us. Nothing that interested me. I'd known those boys since I was nine years old, and aside from Ezra Adams they all still pretty much behaved the same way now as they had when I'd first met them. Except now they burped louder and offered each other congratulations instead of jeers.

Anyway, I felt safest when I was walking with Mr. Craig. While I might take a position on the pro side of the gun control issue for a session of our mock congress in government class, I knew I'd feel a whole lot more secure behind Mr. Craig's handgun if a bear charged us than I would feel behind even the largest canister of concentrated pepper spray.

So whether Mr. Craig would choose to speak to me again or not, I hurried to catch up with him.

My father fingered the empty tent sack I'd flung over a branch and cautiously addressed Madison and me. "Can I give you ladies a hand?"

Madison glanced from him to me and finally down at the heap of blue material and plastic and metal poles at our feet.

It was the tent Madison and Rachel were going to be sharing. Since I'd already helped Jacy put ours up, she had recruited me to assist Madison while she brought the first-aid kit over to Rachel and showed her how to take care of blisters. But Madison might as well have had a stump for a teacher. I couldn't even be sure that I'd chosen a decent enough piece of ground to put the tent on, let alone set it up.

"Please," Madison said to my father even as she shrugged apologetically at me.

I looked over my shoulder at the spot where my father had been getting his tent out of its pouch only moments before and grimaced to see it fully set up and staked down already.

"It's pretty easy once you've done it a couple times," he said.

"Secret of strength number six," Madison said to me, "is to recognize when you need to ask for help and to ask for it from someone who won't steer you wrong."

I recognized that we needed help, all right. I just didn't particularly want it from my father. But I didn't want to make a scene either. And he obviously knew how to set up a dome tent.

"We'd appreciate that, yeah," I said to him. To Madison, I said, "Secret number six? What are you talking about?"

"My Dad and I came up with a list of seven secrets to having inner strength, which he says I'll need if I'm going to find myself still serving God after my teenage years." She shrugged. "I think he's calmed down a little now that we're in a small town."

Billings? A small town? It was a city of nearly one hundred thousand people! "I bet Jacy and Dakota don't think of Billings as a small town," I said.

"Well, compared to Chicago it is."

I had to concede to that. But not to the idea that teens in Billings might somehow face fewer temptations to stray from and distractions to lure them away from their focus on God just because there were fewer people around. I suspected that even Jacy and Dakota, way up here in the middle of nowhere, had their own share of temptations and distractions to battle. Theirs might be different from those of the average teen in Chicago or even Billings, but they'd have some nonetheless. It was just the way of the world. And of our enemy. And of our own sinful natures.

I glanced at my father as he explained how we'd crisscross the poles across the dome-shaped tent, clip them in the plastic hooks that ran along the seams, and then bend them to put their tips through the metal-ringed holes at the base of the tent. I'd known full well since the day he'd showed up at our house that God would want me to forgive him. That God would want and maybe even expect restoration in our relationship. I'd known, and still did know, that moving forward instead of continuing to empower the past would be beneficial for everyone involved, including myself.

But I'd wanted to be and stay angry. I'd wanted to fight what God wanted with everything in me.

None of that had anything to do with living in a city or a small town or no town at all. It had to do with what was inside myself. And everyone had to deal with that.

"So what are your seven secrets?" I asked Madison.

Dad stopped unrolling the rainfly to hear her answer.

"Number one is to read the Bible so that you know what God expects," Madison said. "Number two is to do what God expects even when you don't feel like it. Number three is to get your mind out of its own little world as frequently as possible. We used to help out at rescue missions and stuff like that." She shrugged. "It gave us the chance to tell and show other people about Jesus and to see Him work in their lives, which would supposedly increase our faith in Him for our own lives."

"And did it?" my father asked.

"Yeah," she said. "It does. Number four is to call sin *sin*, and to never think that a little bit won't hurt you because a little bit usually leads to a little bit more which usually leads to a lot."

"Like drugs and stuff," I said, nodding.

"Yeah, that," Madison said, "and things like cussing and lying and watching movies that have a little bit of sin in them or listening to music that talks about bad stuff. I might think it's not going to hurt me, but it gets in my brain, and like the Word says, it's what's already inside the man that defiles him. So why put in more junk?"

"And you actually live by all these secrets?" I asked.

She laughed. "I wish. I fight them just like any other kid. But I'm kind of figuring out that I usually end up regretting it when I do."

The three of us stretched the rainfly over the tent and tied it down.

Then I stood up and had to grin. Another tent stood ready for use in front of me. I'd had my hands on it during each step of the process of getting it that way, and I'd had detailed instructions. Still, I'd managed to retain almost none of the information or experience and had no doubt that I'd be just as useless the next night when it came time to set up camp.

Oh well. Madison would remember. She'd be able to do it with her eyes closed before too long. In fact, she'd probably be ready to be a mountain guide herself by the end of this hike.

"So what are the rest of your secrets?" I asked her.

My father stayed to hear them too.

"Number five is to only do stuff you'd still do if Jesus was standing right next to you. I already told you what number six was. And number seven we got from a bumper sticker we saw."

"A bumper sticker?" My father laughed.

Madison laughed too. "Crazy, huh? But, hey, if it works, why not?"

"So what's the secret?" I pressed. "This great piece of wisdom gleaned from the bumper of a car?"

"It was an SUV actually," Madison said. "Anyway, number seven is to always remember that there is a God, and that you are not Him."

"Fair enough," I said. "Sounds like you and your dad thought of pretty much everything."

It also sounded like Madison and her father were very close, but I didn't mention that.

My father busied himself with helping Payne and Rizzo set up their tent. Madison busied herself with a book she'd brought along. Several of the boys along with Pastor Adams and Jacy and Mr. Craig busied themselves fishing at the shore of the lake and along the creek that ran into it. And I busied myself trying to find a comfortable place to sit and do nothing.

It was a challenge.

Boulders were too hard to sit on for very long, and even if they hadn't been, once a person stopped moving for more than three and a half seconds, mosquitoes came around to dine. Not many at once, but enough to be thoroughly annoying. I thought about going inside the tent to get away from them, but didn't because I hadn't hiked all the way up to this beautiful lake to sit inside my tent.

So I sat on a boulder, did my best to keep the mosquitoes from getting too much of a feast at my expense, and watched people fish.

Not exactly exciting, but pleasant enough. The late afternoon sun shone down bright and steady against my sweatshirt, but a cool breeze carrying the scent of pine and of bug spray and of someone else's campfire kept the warmth from becoming oppressive.

I turned to grin at my father as he passed by behind me heading away from camp. "Didn't do enough walking for one day?" I called out to him.

He smiled, probably surprised that I'd initiated conversation. "I'm going to start collecting firewood," he said. Then he paused to move a rock with the toe of his boot. "I could use a hand if you're not doing anything."

"Well," I said, getting to my feet. "I'm not doing anything, so . . . sure."

I followed him out of the clearing where we'd made camp into the thick trees surrounding it. As we walked, I bent and picked up dried sticks and twigs, and my father used a small handsaw to cut bigger branches from a fallen and graying tree.

We didn't talk. Not even about the trail. But after four or five trips into the trees, we'd piled up enough wood near the circle of stones Mr. Craig had set up as our fire site that my father figured we could quit.

"Hayden's not planning to have a fire in the morning," he told me, "and this ought to be plenty for tonight."

"Great," I said.

We stood on either side of the woodpile for several moments, my father repositioning some of the bigger logs with his boot and me pulling nervously at a couple of splinters I'd gotten in my palm. It didn't seem right to walk away from him without saying anything, but I didn't know what to say. I suspected that maybe he was struggling with the same sense of awkwardness.

He was the first to conquer it, if so. "I'm glad you decided not to go home," he said quietly.

"Me too," I said after a while.

He pointed at my feet. "Nice boots."

I glanced down at them and smiled nervously. The boots were obviously new. Stylish. Chosen without his help.

And distinctly uncomfortable.

After only one day of fairly easy hiking—at least that was how Mr. Craig had described it—I could already feel the burning of blisters on the outside of my left little toe and the inside of my right big toe.

Of course I had no intention of admitting that to my father. I opened my mouth to acknowledge his comment with something vague like thanks or yeah I like them too, but he spoke more quickly.

"They should be good and broken in by the end of this hike," he said.

I shoved my hands into my pockets and kicked at the dirt at my feet.

"In the meantime," he said, "it'll help to take them off in camp and soak your feet in the cold lake water."

The urge to squint questioningly at him as if my feet felt just fine and I had no idea why he'd suggest I'd want to soak them tempted me, but I declined. "I'll do that," I told my father. "Thanks."

CHAPTER 09

Later that first night on the trail after we'd finished dinner and had hung our packs in trees a couple hundred yards downwind of camp, I sat near the campfire huddled in all three of my sweatshirts between Dakota Craig and Pastor Adams. Sparks snapped from the burning logs and rose on the air and smoke toward the moonlit sky.

"It's a clear night," Mr. Craig said. "We'll be able to see the stars in a little while."

"Even with the moon so bright?" I asked.

"Yeah," Dakota said. "Especially if you walk a little ways from the fire."

I glanced at Dakota and wondered if he was ever afraid in the mountains at night. For me, the thought of walking even five feet from our circle around the fire stood hair up on my arms. Our tents were only a few yards away, and I could barely see them against the dense darkness of the trees behind them. I supposed my eyes might adjust to the moonlit night once I'd stepped away from the firelight, but I didn't plan on testing that supposition. Not unless Dakota or Ezra or one of their fathers or even my father offered to accompany me.

"I'm sure the stars are something to see up here," I said.

"Nothing like it anywhere else I've been," Dakota said.

"And that's all of two or three places," his sister teased.

"Are you making any vacation plans for this year?" Pastor Adams asked Mr. Craig.

"Don't know yet," he answered.

Something howled from somewhere up above us and off in the direction of our backpacks.

Rachel startled and then looked straight across the flames at Mr. Craig. "Wolves?"

He shook his head. "Coyotes. Nothing to worry about."

I thought about the thin translucent material of our dome tents and then of all the animals that could conceivably be wandering the wilderness at night.

It seemed to me like plenty to worry about, but I didn't say so. Mr. Craig hadn't spoken directly to me since our little confrontation on the trail, and I wasn't about to force him to speak just to have him disagree with me, and probably irritably too.

As the night grew later and colder, people began to grab their flashlights and leave in groups for their tents. First three of the boys. Then two more. Then Rachel and Madison. Then Ezra and Pastor Adams.

I wouldn't have minded going to bed for the night. The thought of curling up in a ball in my sleeping bag was entirely appealing. But I was sharing a tent with Jacy and there was no way I was going to head there without her. She seemed more than happy to stay near the fire with her father and brother.

And with my father.

For a while the five of us left at the fire chatted about other trails in the area and old mining roads, but when it had gone silent for a while, Jacy leaned her elbows on her knees and stared intently at my father. "So you did mountain rescue, Mr. Benjamin?"

My father looked cautiously over at me and then back at Jacy. "Yes."

I could tell by the way Jacy kept staring at him that she was eager to hear more, but she didn't press him when he failed to say more.

"Just so we're clear," Mr. Craig said to him, "I'll be grateful for your help should we need it, but if you and me disagree after weighing all our options, we do it my way."

I felt oddly put out on my father's behalf. Judging by what Mr. Craig himself had said about his experience as a mountain guide, he'd never officially done organized rescue work. My father certainly possessed more experience and training. Mr. Craig should be thankful to have him along instead of asserting his own less qualified male ego.

But my father replied, "Absolutely," without hesitation and as easily as if Mr. Craig had done nothing more than remark about the weather. "That's the way of it."

Mr. Craig nodded. "You'd be surprised how many guys can't understand that."

My father grinned. "You'd be surprised how much wouldn't surprise me."

Both men laughed.

Then they talked. For nearly two hours. About the trails they'd hiked. The tests of nature they'd encountered. Certain memorable idiots they'd guided, and in my father's case, rescued. The times they figured they'd have done something differently if they had it to do over again. What they loved about the mountains.

Jacy sat intently on the edge of the log she'd been sitting on all evening, savoring every word. It was obvious that she loved the stories themselves, but I didn't doubt that her enjoyment of them had more to do with the openness with which the two men told them. There was no question in my mind after a day and a half of watching Jacy and her father that she was both protected by him and protective of him. Watching her watch him as he settled into relaxed conversation was a bit like watching a child stare in simple appreciation at an unexpected gift.

I caught myself staring at my father after a while, wishing that I knew his stories already as Jacy knew her father's. Wishing I could feel as safe in his presence as Jacy clearly felt in Mr. Craig's. Wishing there was nothing more separating us than the campfire we were sitting on opposite sides of. Wishing . . . and feeling helpless to make any of it happen or even to accept it if my father or God or someone else found a way to hold the possibility out to me.

But I did pay attention to my father's stories and to the impressions I got about him from the things he chose to elaborate on or laugh about or that made him go quiet. By the time I left the fire to go have a look at the stars with Dakota, I'd concluded that if he'd been a stranger sitting at the campfire instead of the father who had abandoned me, I would have liked him. He was funny and articulate. Brave too—if his stories were true. I would have come to the conclusion that he'd chosen such a difficult and lonely life to try to hide away from some secret woundedness, and I would probably have spent hours afterward in my tent trying to come up with scenarios that might account for that woundedness.

But he wasn't a stranger. And he had been the one doing the wounding all the years he was hiding away in Alaska. Even as he was saving other people's lives.

I ran into Dakota's hand in front of me and stopped short just before I would have walked face first into a snarl of branches. "Thanks," I muttered to him. "Too busy looking at the ground in the flashlight beam, I guess."

He took firm hold of my elbow and led me out of the trees and down to a flat boulder near the shore of the lake. Reflected moonlight hopped on the peaks of the gentle waves and made the rock seem almost to glow.

"It's so pretty," I said.

"Wait till you see this." Dakota pulled on my elbow until I sat down. "Lie back and look straight up."

When I did, he stepped several feet away from me onto another huge rock and did the same.

Even though the rock felt like ice beneath me and even though I felt somewhat vulnerable to any wild creature that might spy me from the trees and lumber over to investigate, I stared in complete amazement at the stars. It seemed as if my eyes would just get focused on them, and then I'd realize there were more behind the ones I was looking at, and then more behind them until forever.

"Pretty awesome, huh?" Dakota asked me as he got to his feet again, jumped from his rock to mine, and then held his hand out to me.

I grabbed his hand and let him help me up. "Sure is."

"You'll never see that in the city," he said.

"Unless there's a blackout."

He held my elbow as we entered the trees again and started walking back toward the fire. "Not even then on account of the smog," he said.

I didn't think Billings had that much smog, but I didn't argue with Dakota. It probably did have enough to hinder a person from getting a clear view of the stars. Besides, the experience was too special, too unique, to waste even the tiniest portion of it arguing.

"Thanks for taking me over there," I told Dakota.

"No problem," he said. "To tell you the truth, I was getting kind of bored of mountain stories."

I laughed.

"It was good to see Dad talk so much," he said. "He's usually pretty quiet. Keeps to himself."

"That's what Jacy said." I shrugged. "It's probably just because he and my father have mountain guiding in common."

"Yeah," he said. Then he laughed. "And you know, if one of them was in a major thunderstorm, then the other is obligated to point out the time he was in a blizzard, and then—"

"If one of them was attacked by a six-hundred-pound grizzly, then—"

"The other was stalked by a pack of wolves."

"The male ego," I said.

Dakota said, "Hey," and then stopped walking to playfully tap my head with his flashlight. "Ego or not," he said once we'd started walking again, "all my dad's stories are true. I was there for most of them. How about your dad's?"

"I wouldn't know for sure," I said quietly.

"You two aren't too close, are you?" he asked me.

"No."

Dakota listened quietly as we made our way through the thickest trees toward the fire that we could see clearly now as I told him about my father's leaving and showing up again. Just before we stepped into the clearing where Mr. Craig had set up the fire ring and where we'd pitched our tents, he squeezed my elbow gently until I stopped walking and turned to face him in the goldish dark. "That's rough," he said.

"Well, not as rough as one of my parents dying," I said, feeling ashamed and suddenly aware of how cold I had become since leaving the fire. "I shouldn't be whining to you, Dakota."

"You weren't whining," he said. "But you're right in one way. You still have the opportunity to have your father in your life. Give him a chance to explain the past." He shrugged. "If he's like my father, he wouldn't have hurt you for the world if he could've seen any way around it."

"He could have written a letter," I whispered.

Dakota stood still and silent for several seconds. Then he smiled and said, "Unless he was stranded up on some peak with wolves on one side and an impending avalanche on the other and couldn't get to the post office to mail anything."

I knew what Dakota was trying to do and I appreciated it. I did. But I didn't want the situation lightened or put into some kind of supposed objective perspective or tucked away behind the laughter of a previous and easier conversation.

In nine years' time my father could have sent a card. No matter what.

"Or maybe," Dakota added more seriously, "that's how he felt on the inside."

I had not thought of that. "Like no matter what he did, it wouldn't help?"

"Yeah," Dakota said. "Since he'd already climbed the peak."

"That was his choice."

"I know." Dakota stepped away from me to acknowledge his father's greeting and click off his flashlight. Before he joined his father near the fire, though, he turned to me again. "So was coming back."

CHAPTER

Noon pressed down on us hot and unrelenting the next day, and I stopped on the so-called trail to wipe sweat off my face with my arm. I'd learned from hard experience that the sunscreen and insect repellent I'd rubbed and sprayed all over every patch of exposed skin did not agree with my eyes, so I was careful to avoid them now.

"You okay?" Mr. Craig called to me from above.

"Couldn't be better," I mumbled.

"This is the only rough spot," he reminded me for the third time.

"Got it," I said.

But the truth was that I didn't have it at all. And that I wondered how anything could be rougher than our last forty minutes of hiking through mud and stumps and a hill that had kept pretty much even with my nose the whole way up. And, on top of everything, this was not just a rough spot on the trail. There wasn't even a trail! It had been washed out decades ago by a rockslide, and nobody had bothered to clean it up.

Of course, how would they? The boulders we were trying to navigate our way up, around, and over had to weigh several hundred pounds apiece. And the whole side of the mountain, including the trail that had switchbacked its way peacefully up it, lay powdered beneath them.

Mr. Craig stepped to the edge of the boulder I was trying to figure out how to climb without the weight of my pack pulling me backwards and down. "Need a hand?"

"No," I shouted up to him. *Leave me alone, will you?*

"Suit yourself," he said and stepped away from the edge and out of my view, but not before I noticed his amused smile.

I stared at the boulder in front of me.

I looked around for a way to bypass it, but it was the smallest boulder in sight. And it was solidly wedged between two others. Many of the boulders in this chute moved when people attempted to step on them.

Scary.

"Grab the top and put the toe of your boot in that crack halfway up," a voice said behind me.

My father.

"I'm right behind you," he said. "But you won't need me."

Leaning my head back and blowing a long breath out through my lips, I shut my eyes and tried to calm my rushed breathing and edgy emotion. Then, without stopping to think or question, I did what my father had instructed.

Once I'd gotten my balance on top of the boulder, I gave Mr. Craig a hasty thumbs-up and then wiped my palms on the front of my jeans. They were sweaty. And dirty.

When my father made his way easily onto the boulder behind me, I thanked him for his help and then plowed full force into conquering the next boulder.

And the next.

And the next.

Until we'd reached the top of the chute and stood on a solidly packed trail again and could see the huge high mountain lake below us. Lower Aero Lake. Its color looked almost navy blue against the short grasses and rocks that surrounded it.

"Whew," I whispered. "Pretty."

"Sure is," Mr. Craig said, moving to stand right beside me. "It's rare to see high mountain lakes the size of this one. It's more than a mile long." He turned to address the rest of the group when they'd all gathered around us. "Anyone need a break?"

"No way," Madison answered. "Let's just get away from that thing."

Several of us laughed.

But an undeniable sense of accomplishment quickened my pace all that afternoon and enabled me to volunteer to help my father gather firewood that evening instead of waiting to be asked or hoping he'd recruit someone else. It was a more challenging job than it had been the night before since Lower Aero Lake sat above the tree line where only scrubby little bushes grew, but we managed it.

Except for the fact that I was beginning to feel dirty and that my feet hurt, the afternoon and evening could not have been more perfect.

Dinner was satisfying. Big brook trout cooked in squeeze butter served with slightly rubberized backpacking food . . . rice pilaf. The taste and texture of the trout more than made up for that which the rice lacked.

Sunset came and turned to darkness with beautiful peace and stillness.

And I wasn't even afraid after a couple hours sitting near the fire to go to my tent ahead of Jacy. She'd be there soon enough.

It had been a strenuous day, and I had no doubt that I'd fall asleep quickly and stay that way till morning.

But at some point during the darkest part of night, I awoke because something was pushing at the side of my tent.

Right next to my head.

I could hear Jacy breathing beside me. I could hear the still-ness and knew that meant everyone had turned in for the night. I could no longer see the glow of the fire through the side of the tent that faced it.

The side of the tent that now moved again as something pressed up next to it.

I had no idea what to do.

Jacy had our canister of pepper spray, but I didn't know where she had put it. If I moved to look for it, the thing outside would surely hear me and . . .

What if it was a bear?

Or a wolf?

I lay perfectly still.

Until a low growl made its way closer to me.

Then I screamed.

I couldn't help it.

It just came out, like a hapless cat out of a yard with a dog in it.

Jacy sat up beside me, felt around her feet for her flashlight, and whispered, "Lay back down, Taren. Now."

I obeyed.

"Dad!" she called out.

I heard a tent zipper, then laughter, and then shouting.

"What are you thinking?"

"I'm sorry," the laughter-tightened voice right beside our tent said. "You should have heard Taren scr—"

"I did hear Taren scream," said the other voice outside, a man's voice, a voice tightened by anger.

Mr. Craig.

"Lucky for you I'm not a trigger-happy person. Or maybe you figure I'd just come out rubbing my eyes and saying howdy to Smokey?"

The boy outside my tent—and now I recognized his voice too, Payne the Pain—kept laughing.

Beside me, Jacy pulled in a long breath and then lay back. "Why are there always idiots?" she muttered into her sleeping bag as she pulled it over her head.

"Go back to bed, Payne," I said. My heart had begun to beat so thickly that I could feel its pounding in my ears.

"Are you all right, Taren?" Mr. Craig asked me.

"Yes, sir." I still couldn't pull in a decent breath, but I decided that Mr. Craig didn't need to know that. "I'm sorry I screamed," I told him. "I'm sure that was the wrong thing to do. Especially if it had been a bear or whatever."

"It's understandable," Mr. Craig said.

Payne finally managed to quit laughing. I heard him get to his feet beside my tent. "I'm sorry," he said.

"You're sorry, all right," Mr. Craig said. "And you would have been a lot more sorry if I'd have shot you. Go back to your tent."

Payne went without another word and without any more laughter.

"Could he have shot him?" I whispered to Jacy after a while. When everything had gone quiet again.

"He never shoots without knowing what he's shooting first," she said. "He was just making a point." Then she laughed a little. "I should have poked my can of pepper spray out the door and hit him with a burst of it just to teach him a lesson."

"I figure he's learned his lesson," I said.

Jacy stayed quiet for several seconds. Then she rolled onto her side and pulled her knees up to her stomach. "I hope so."

Well, if the next day of hiking was any indication, the only lesson Payne had learned was that the mountains offered him a whole new repertoire of potential pranks. He feigned at least three heart attacks, hid in the bushes and howled like a wolf to try to scare Rachel, fell on his face twice while trying to dance among the boulders, and stuck his own hand with a fishhook when we'd taken a break along the creek.

But the day was perfect. Sunny but not overly warm. Just enough of a breeze to keep the bugs manageable. The hike itself was challenging because of the boulders all along the ground and a couple of creeks we had to cross—one of them wide enough that there was no way to avoid getting our feet wet even with all the rocks sticking up through its surface. But it remained fairly level, and we could plainly see at all times where we were heading. We could see the huge vertical side of Granite Peak, the highest point in Montana, as we walked. And we were left to envision the mountains that stood obscured from our view because of it, including one called Froze to Death Plateau.

I understood then what Jacy had meant about the trail being eerie. The area was so huge. So many forgotten and windswept boulders.

Eerie.

And ancient.

I did what I could to busy my mind since my own breathlessness at the top of the mountain prevented my being able to talk to anyone.

I wondered what all the mosquitoes survived on when we weren't around.

I wondered about the men who had discovered and named these lakes . . . and Froze to Death Plateau.

I wondered at the fact that we were actually only covering a couple of miles that day even though the strain of the altitude more than adequately convinced my body that we were hiking much farther.

I thought about the true story Mr. Craig had told us that morning when we'd set out about a man named John Colter. He'd been a member of the Lewis and Clark expedition but had decided to stay in the mountains at its conclusion instead of heading back east. He and a buddy, whose name was Potts, had been in a canoe trapping beaver on the other side of the Beartooths when they were attacked by a band of warriors from the Blackfeet tribe. They killed Colter's friend in front of him, stripped Colter of his clothes and possessions, and asked him in English if he was a fast runner. He'd lied and told them he wasn't, so they set him in a field and told him to run. He saw trees in the distance and knew there'd be a river there, so he ran the two miles toward it. He was a fast runner after all, but he had no shoes on and the rocks on the earth began to tear his feet. Still, the warriors struggled to catch him. When one did, he threw his spear at Colter but missed, so Colter used it to kill him and then continued toward the river. He dove in when he got there and found shelter and air underneath a beaver dam, where he stayed until the warriors quit searching for him. Then he ran for eleven days and two hundred miles until he found a trapper's station in the wilderness where he could get some clothes and be assured of safety from his pursuers. Later, Colter became the first white man to investigate the Native American accounts of a land of fire, and was the first to see the geysers in what is now Yellowstone National Park. For quite a while prior to it becoming a national park, though, people referred to the place as Colter's Hell because of the descriptions of it that he sent back east.

"This area has a lot of colorful characters in its past," Mr. Craig had concluded almost proudly when he'd finished his story. "That campground near my place was named for Colter."

I'd wondered then if there'd be a campground named for Mr. Ezekiel Crenshaw someday. Or even one for Hayden Craig.

But then I'd concluded that if one had to run barefoot and naked through the Beartooth Wilderness in order to have a campground named for him, both men would probably be content to live and die without the honor. Especially poor Mr. Crenshaw with his weary knees.

The lake we camped near that night was tiny. Not even on the official map of the wilderness area. But it was beautiful. Especially at sunset.

Lone Elk Lake.

I wondered how this lake had earned its name. Had some cartographer stumbled upon it, possibly at sunset, to startle a lone elk standing majestically at its shore?

I mentioned my thought to Madison only to receive a curious squint, as if she thought I'd had a little too much thinking time on my hands that day.

But then, the overall mood of the evening was slightly tense because Payne the Pain had decided to catch one of the big cutthroat trout with his bare hands and had fallen into the frigid water. Mr. Craig had gotten him out right away and had built as large a fire as the area's sparse wood-stuffs would permit, but Payne still shivered and complained and apologized to an annoying fault, and everyone ended up turning in for the night early.

It was just as well. I was tired and felt certain I could count on a good night's sleep.

Payne the Pain would not be playing bear or anything else that night.

CHAPTER 11

We awoke the next morning to cold wind. We packed up camp quickly and ate our breakfast, granola bars, as we hiked. Clouds hung overhead all day, turning the sky and the scenery dull even as it seemed to accentuate the area's rugged and untamed harshness. It rained intermittently on us as we walked. Sometimes in random drops. Sometimes in wind-powered torrents that tore at our clear plastic rain ponchos and at our good humor. Late in the afternoon, it hailed on us. Pea-sized hail mostly, but a few of the stones were bigger, and all of them pelted into us on the cold strength of the wind.

Not a pleasant experience.

We were well above tree line. Even the scrubby little bushes didn't grow at this altitude. There was absolutely no place to take shelter in, not even for a couple minutes. So we kept walking, hoping the disagreeable weather would clear out by the time we arrived at Sky Top Lakes so that we wouldn't have to attempt to get our tents up in the wind and rain.

As we passed by the seemingly eternal shore of Upper Aero Lake, the ground itself seemed to shift and change in layers. First gray granite. Then white granite speckled with black. Then green granite. Then black granite speckled with white.

My face and hands were numb from the cold, and my eyes were exhausted from squinting against the wind all day when I ran into my father on the trail.

Literally.

"Sorry," I muttered to him.

"Stay right behind me," he said to me, yelling almost to be heard clearly above the noise of the wind and of our two rain ponchos flapping in it.

I nodded and followed right behind him, my face nearly touching his pack.

It did help. A little.

But when the bigger hail came just as we topped a hill and could see the grouping of lakes below us on the other side and still far away enough to be thoroughly discouraging, I felt completely alone and vulnerable and exposed even though my father stood fewer than three inches from me.

Hail dumped from the sky in ice-cube-sized chunks as if some giant invisible hand above us had suddenly tipped a massive bin of ice.

Cold. Hard. Stinging.

It hit us. It bounced off the rocks around us. It plinked against our metal pack frames. It crunched beneath our feet as we kept walking.

It sounded like a sky full of unopened soda cans crashing onto tile.

Ahead of me on the trail, Mr. Craig turned and signaled to everyone to stop and crouch down facing east so that our backpacks would take the brunt of the onslaught.

That helped. Some.

But not nearly as much as when my father pulled me close to him and sheltered my head with his body. His rain poncho felt cold and wet against my cheek, but I could feel his heat and his heartbeat beneath it. The rate of his heartbeat was much slower than mine, I couldn't help noticing. Undoubtedly because his body had grown accustomed to these higher altitudes and to hiking with a pack on his back during his years in Alaska.

The thought of him being in Alaska when he should have been home with Mom and me made me feel cold even as his warmth surrounded and protected me.

I began to cry.

He had to know I was crying because my shoulders shook with my sobbing, and I kept having to reach up and swipe at my nose, but he didn't say anything to me. He only held me more tightly and then let go of me without a word to get stiffly to his feet when the hail finally quit.

"Is everyone all right?" Mr. Craig wanted to know.

Everyone said that they were, but I could see a cut on Pastor Adams' face and a bruise forming at the corner of Payne the Pain's left eye.

That felt a little too much like divine justice to me, since I'd been wanting to punch Payne for two whole days for scaring me at Lower Aero Lake, and I had to smile.

And then I shook my head. My emotions had become as ragged as the torn hem of my rain poncho.

But the sky cleared gradually so that by the time we set up camp in a green grassy meadow the appropriate distance from the shore of the longest and skinniest of the Sky Top lakes, the sun had melted a hollow for itself in the thin clouds at the edge of the storm and kept shining until it stood alone in clear bright blue.

Just in time to eat the golden trout that Mr. Craig, Pastor Adams, Ezra, and my father had caught and cooked.

Golden trout were rare, Mr. Craig had told us. And they were beautiful. Shimmering gold with brown ovals running down the sides and black fins with white tips.

But after a day of hiking, especially the day we'd had, and with the alternative of eating only backpacking food, even more important than their being beautiful was the fact that the golden trout were delicious.

"This is so good," Madison said around a mouthful of it.

"It's because you're starved," Payne said, "because we didn't stop for lunch."

Madison shook her head. "This is good because it's good."

I smiled at Mr. Craig's smile.

"Can we hike up that peak?" Rizzo asked Pastor Adams as he pointed across the lake at the rest of the mountain rising up from its opposite shore.

Pastor Adams glanced at Mr. Craig who said, "Sure. Just be careful. Rocks might be slick after all the rain."

Getting permission turned out to be the easy part for Rizzo. Finding people who felt like hiking with him presented much more of a challenge.

"No way," Ezra said when Rizzo looked in his direction. "I'm wiped out after today's hike."

"Me too," Dakota told him.

"Don't even look at me," I said.

Everyone laughed.

But then Payne the Pain said he'd go—probably just to get away from Mr. Craig, who'd been glaring at him at every possible opportunity.

Including now.

"Just don't decide you're going to pretend to be an eagle and fly up there," he said to Payne.

I watched Jacy gently reprimand her father with her elbow in his ribs, and I watched her father glare at Payne anyway, and I laughed.

Then Jacy glared at me.

"Stay where you can see us," Pastor Adams told the boys who finally walked away from our campfire. "And head back before it starts getting dark."

"Yes, sir," Payne said, saluting.

Mr. Craig glared a moment longer and then turned to Pastor Adams. "And you enjoy working with these people?"

Pastor Adams grinned. "Mostly."

"Payne's just a pain," Madison said around another mouthful of fish, and we all laughed.

Even Mr. Craig. Until his expression went serious again and he said, "Don't most churches have a pastor just to work with the kids so that the main guy doesn't have to?"

Amusement showed in Pastor Adams' eyes. "Hayden," he said, "I like working with the kids. But yes, most churches have a youth pastor. Someone who is especially called to work with teens. We've had different guys do it from time to time in our church, but two of them moved on to foreign missions, one of them took the head pastorate of one of our fellowship's churches in North Dakota, and the last one decided to go to Bible college." He shrugged. "So, I do it in between all the interims."

"We've got a new guy coming in the fall," Ezra told Mr. Craig. "But Dad does just as good a job."

"I have a great youth staff," Pastor Adams clarified.

"It'd be fun to go to a youth group," Jacy said.

This earned her father's attention. He stopped shoving sticks into the fire to sit up straight and look at her.

"It would be good to have friends my own age who believed in God and stuff," she explained to him.

"It'd be good to have friends my own age, period," Dakota said, laughing a little.

Mr. Craig didn't laugh, though. He leaned forward toward the fire and stared down at the burning sticks and brush.

"But I wouldn't trade our life," Dakota said quietly.

Mr. Craig lifted his head and looked at Jacy.

She didn't notice. She was preoccupied telling Madison and Rachel how fortunate they were to have one another as friends and to have the whole youth group to be close to and to do things with.

I looked around the fire at the kids from our youth group. I supposed that they did do stuff together, but I didn't think that any of them were particularly close. Rachel had her plans for the future. Madison had her gymnastics. Rizzo had his computer nerd friends from his school. Corey had his popular crowd friends from his. Payne the Pain didn't have any friends from any school. Ezra tended to stick with his father whenever he had the choice.

And me?

Well, I was only here in these mountains with this youth group because I'd wanted to get away from my father . . . who was sitting right there across the fire from me.

Maybe the new youth pastor would be able to pull this mismatched group of kids onto some kind of common ground, but it would be a challenge. The previous youth pastor hadn't succeeded in accomplishing it. Neither had Pastor Adams, and he was about as good a leader as anyone could hope to find.

I suspected that he was counting on our time in the mountains, pulling together to master a mutual challenge and all that, to unite us kids. At least a little.

So far, it didn't seem to be working.

Of course, the mountains had yet to throw anything truly perilous at us. The rock chute had been tough, but the adults had done most of the helping while we kids had pretty much stood around and laughed at one another. The hail had attacked us, but other than my father and me, everyone had endured the storm alone with only a backpack for protection.

"Youth group is all right," Madison was saying to Jacy when their conversation pushed its way into my awareness again, interrupting an eerie barrage of scenarios that might conceivably come up and force us to work together—none of which I cared to experience. "But you get to meet all kinds of different people from all over the place."

Jacy nodded. "That is fun." Now she looked at her father. "And I love living up here and working with Dad." She smiled. "Even if I do have to put up with idiots pretending to be bears once in a while."

Mr. Craig nodded and began repositioning sticks in the fire again.

"Speaking of Payne," my father said, pointing past me to the jagged peak of boulders and loose earth rising up on the other side of the lake, "do you suppose he ought to be doing that?"

We all turned to watch Payne push a huge boulder from its perch atop another one. It smacked against a couple of the larger boulders near it and then bounced down the hill, taking many smaller rocks and a lot of dirt with it into the lake at the bottom with a noisy splash.

Even after the sound of the splash and its echo subsided, small rocks kept making their way down the slope.

"Nope," Mr. Craig said, getting to his feet. "He probably ought not to be doing that."

Pastor Adams stood too and followed Mr. Craig to the shore, and the two men walked together toward the inlet.

I sat for a long while near the fire. Watching the flames. Smelling the smoke. Enjoying its warmth. The calm feel of evening settled in around us before darkness did. Most of the people stayed near the fire talking, but when my father stood and walked down to the lakeshore, I followed him.

I wasn't sure why, and I hoped he wouldn't ask.

He didn't.

"Ever skipped rocks on the water?" he asked me when I'd stopped to stand beside him.

Light from the setting sun touched the peaks of the lake's many small waves. They seemed to dance in the middle of the lake in a million glittery skirts. By the time they reached shore, though, the spotlight had abandoned them back to their perfect clearness.

"No," I told my father.

He bent to sort through the rocks at his feet. When he stood again, holding a small flat rock out toward me, he said, "Watch the water."

I obeyed.

He flung the rock straight past his hip just like I'd seen many kids toss a Frisbee. It hit the water and bounced off it again. Once. Twice. Three times. Four.

"Wow," I said. "That's cool. Show me how you did it."

So for the next half-hour or more, my father and I stood at the shore of Sky Top Lake and skipped rocks on its choppy, glistening waves. We laughed at my first embarrassing attempts, and then congratulated one another on our increasingly accurate tosses.

I tossed one rock that skipped ten times on the waves before it disappeared into the water, but the record when we'd used up all the flat rocks within reach belonged to my father. He'd tossed a rock that had skipped twelve times before sinking.

"It smells so clean up here," I said when we'd been standing side by side for quite a while without speaking.

"I love that about the mountains," he said.

"So . . . so did you go to Alaska right after you left Billings?" I asked him.

Hadn't Dakota encouraged me to give my father a chance to explain the past? Yes. And didn't I deserve an explanation? Definitely. But more than either of those things, I simply wanted to know.

I wanted to know more about the man beside me. My father. I wanted to know why he'd chosen to go to Alaska. How he'd gotten there. How he'd found work there and with whom. I wanted to know how he'd gotten the scar beneath his right eye and why he seemed to limp a little when he got tired. I wanted to know where he'd lived and what the place had looked like and if he'd hung my picture on the wall above his dresser.

"No," he said. "I worked on oil fields in eastern Montana for a while. Out on the ends of the earth, Taren. That's what it's like out there. You can see for miles—only there's nothing to see but plains and sky. Then a buddy of mine went up to Alaska to work on the North Slope and I went with him. I hated the oil work, so I moved into a small village and started running tours with this local guide. That led to running my own tours. I'd fly people in to hunt or what—"

"You know how to fly a plane?"

"The little ones," he said. "But it's not my favorite thing to do." He turned to look directly at me. His eyes held so much intensity, so much emotion, that I almost had to look away from him.

But I didn't.

"Basically, Taren," he said, "I'd do something until it wasn't new anymore because once it wasn't new anymore my thoughts had time to . . . to go back to Billings. To your mother." He licked his lips and turned to look at the water again. "To you."

"Why'd you leave in the first place?" I'd barely had the voice for the question or the courage to be sure I really wanted to know its answer, but I'd had just enough of them both.

"Your mother wasn't happy," he said. "I didn't have the right kind of job or make enough money or think of taking her out to dinner or getting her flowers. And she was right. I didn't. But she complained about it so much and asked me why I couldn't be more like so-and-so-down-the-block's husband and . . . I guess it just made me crazy. I started staying away more and more and taking her out to dinner and getting her flowers less and less, and . . ." He shrugged. "We were fighting all the time. I just didn't know how to make it work. Neither did she. And after a while, neither of us wanted to."

"But you didn't just leave Mom," I said quietly.

"I know."

I watched my father watch the water until I thought I would scream. "That's it? You know? That's all you're going to say to me?"

"What *can* I say, Taren?"

My hands tightened into fists at my sides as I took a step back from my father and stared at him, too disbelieving to think. I might have liked to have shot out some bitter sarcastic comeback. Or to have laughed out loud. Or to have cried. But I couldn't even think. *What can I say, Taren?*

"Listen to me," he said. He stepped toward me, grabbed hold of my arms with his strong hands, and held them even when I tried to pull away. His eyes had gone as fierce as his hold on my arms. "I never wanted to leave you. I didn't know how to leave your mother and not leave you. I didn't want to see you and then have to leave again. Over and over and over. It was just easier—"

"For you, maybe," I whispered.

"It was just easier to stay gone. For both of us is what I told myself. And by the time I realized how wrong I was about that, I'd already been gone too long to . . . to . . ." He shook his head, released my arms, blew air out forcefully through his lips, and turned away from me. "It was wrong. And no matter how I explain it, it's going to stay wrong. I can't change it now." He kept looking at the waves. "Except in turning it over to God once I'd found Him and in hoping that you'll give me a chance to start over."

And that was exactly it, wasn't it? The bottom line? The point of decision? The end of prelude and the start of the here and now?

My father had come as far as he could. He had come all the way up to the point where nothing else was his to decide. He had come back to Mom and me. He had quit running. He had asked for our forgiveness. He had put his hope out in front of us. He had proven that he had changed.

That God had changed him.

Now the choices belonged to me. The ball was in my court. I held the pen in my hand.

Would I forgive my father?

Would I give him the second chance he'd asked for?

Would I put the past behind—water under the bridge, dust in the wind, smoke drifting away on a night breeze, all that—and move forward?

Now that my father and I had spoken, now that I knew his hope and he knew that I knew it, our relationship could not remain uncertain. Undecided. Dancing back and forth between regretful resignation and reconciliation.

The way I saw it, as I watched Mr. Craig and Pastor Adams move out of the path of another boulder Payne had rolled down from the top of his little king-of-the-hill rock pile, I either had to reject my father outright or accept him outright.

No looking back.

No holding grudges.

No second-guessing.

No more running.

For either one of us.

Unfortunately, neither accepting him completely nor rejecting him completely seemed doable.

Not completely.

CHAPTER 13

Mr. Craig surprised me the next morning by telling me to leave my rainfly tied down. I'd gone to my hands and knees in the dirt beside my tent to start unworking the knots even before Jacy had come back up from the lake with our rinsed-off plates. Proud of myself. That's what I was. I finally knew exactly what to do in camp, and I'd gotten into position to do it before anyone else had and before anyone had to ask me.

"We're leaving camp set up here today," Mr. Craig explained. "We'll hike up to the glacier, spend the day, and come back down and camp here again tonight."

"Oh." I stood and dusted the damp morning dirt from my hands. "Sure. That works."

"You'll really be saying that when you're making that last half mile or so of straight uphill to the glacier," he said. "Not having to carry your pack up there works just fine."

I smiled. "Well, at least I knew what I was supposed to do."

"You're settling right in." He grabbed the bill of my baseball cap and pushed it down over my eyes.

That morning in camp turned out to be the most relaxed so far. The sun warmed the air and earth quickly while we slowly put away all our breakfast gear and while we laughed and spoke about a whole lot of nothing.

Some of the guys fished. Madison washed her hair with panful after panful of icy lake water, which Rachel dutifully collected for her. Again and again, she ran to the lake and then hurried back along the mandatory distance one must leave between the edge of the water and the small pool of biodegradable suds that spread out with every splash of water dumped over Madison's hair.

"Oh, that's cold," Madison kept saying. And Rachel kept laughing. Until she decided to wash her hair and it was Madison dumping the water over her head.

I decided I might as well grit my teeth and wash my hair too. It took several minutes and several panfuls of water to get my hair wet enough. I felt heat and my pulse in my temples each time the water hit my head, but I didn't complain as Madison had. Even if I ended up with a headache that lasted all day, it would be worth it to have clean hair.

When I'd finished and had patted my hair dry with one of my clean T-shirts which I then lay over a boulder to dry in the sun, Jacy double braided it and I felt clean and revitalized. Ready to conquer anything. Even Sky Top Glacier.

Madison glanced for the first time at the bottle of shampoo as she handed it back to Jacy.

"Isn't that the stuff we've been using to wash our dishes?" she asked.

Jacy laughed. "Yeah. It cleans clothes, too. And you can brush your teeth with it. You can also—"

"I don't even want to know," Madison said.

"That explains why it's so *un-fragrant*," Rachel said.

Jacy nodded. "Environmentally safe. But, hey, it works."

"How about you?" I asked her, holding the empty pan out toward her. "Want to wash yours? I'll bring your water."

"Sure." As I walked away from her, she leaned forward and began brushing her hair over the back of her head with her fingers.

My hands were numb by the time I'd brought Jacy water enough times for her to finish with her hair. I shuddered at the

82

thought of what it would feel like to accidentally fall into one of these lakes. This one was just barely warm enough to not be frozen. Along the shore across from the inlet, snow still clung to the rocks and dirt and stretched out over the surface of the water.

Cold.

Jacy's hair wasn't long enough to braid, but she allowed me to brush it out for her. As I did, I said, "You know last night when you said you like working up here with your dad?"

"Yeah?"

"Do you really?"

She laughed. "Yeah."

"You don't mind sleeping on the ground so much and being dirty all the time? Carrying a pack all the time? Always having strange people in your house and cleaning up after them when they've gone?"

She didn't answer right away. When she did, her voice was quiet. "I guess there are times I wish we had a more normal life. You know, getting up in a bed every morning, showering every morning, getting dressed and going to school at a school every morning. Having regular friends who I see every day. Playing sports or whatever after school. Going to church every Sunday. But this is what makes Dad happy, so, yeah, I really do like working up here."

"Aren't you ever scared?" Madison asked her. "Of bears, or someone getting hurt, or of getting lost, or forest fires or whatever?"

"I get scared when I think about someone getting hurt," she said. "The rest of the stuff is pretty much avoidable, but things can happen really fast up here, and someone could get severely hurt in a matter of one careless step. And since that someone would most likely be my dad trying to keep someone else safe . . . yeah, that scares me." She shrugged. "But we've been up here for eight years and have only had one serious injury to a hiker, and that was because she'd brought food into her tent which attracted a bear. Could have been avoided completely if she'd listened to Dad."

"I guess there are scary things to every kind of life," Rachel said. "I mean, getting in your car to drive to the mall could end in a fatal crash."

"Exactly," Jacy said. "And if you live in a city, you have to worry more about crime and random acts of violence and all that."

I handed Jacy her brush over her shoulder. "I guess everything balances out."

"It's not like we climb Mt. Everest every week or someplace like that that's dangerous in and of itself. And it's not like we do those two-hundred-mile adventure races."

"Do you ever want to do that?" Madison asked her.

Jacy laughed. "Are you crazy?"

"What about your dad?" Rachel wanted to know. "Does he?"

"He's never mentioned it. That's a whole different level of hiking and endurance and mountaineering." She stood to her feet, brushed some dirt from the knees of her jeans, and stretched her arms up over her head. "Plus, people train for years before attempting that stuff. That would be way too much like work. This is fun."

I thought of the rock chute we'd climbed that first full day on the trail. It had certainly seemed like work to me. And definitely not fun.

Mr. Craig gathered us all together after a while for the start of our hike to Sky Top Glacier. Only Jacy carried a pack. It contained our lunch, the camp stove, the fuel, the matches, some rope, and the first-aid kit.

Even though we did make better time and covered the miles more quickly than we would have had we been carrying our packs, the hiking was strenuous enough to completely negate the benefits of the lack of weight. Constant uphill. Enough higher up in elevation to make just enough difference in the size and frequency of the appearance of those annoying bright green spots in my vision . . . not to mention leaving me in a perpetual state of gasping. Plus, once again, there was no actual trail. So even though we could plainly see our destination every step of the way, the ground was not smooth or packed or level beneath our feet. Sometimes it was rocky. Sometimes it felt as if we were thumping over a giant hollow drum. Permafrost, Mr. Craig called these grassy sections of the ground. Earth that never quite thawed. Nobody seemed more intrigued by this than Payne, who leaped up and down, stomping and pounding on the ground like an ape.

I wondered if Jacy was still having fun because I sure wasn't.

My father stepped in and walked beside me for a while, but we did not speak.

The glacier ahead of us sat almost like a thick-sided coffee-bean scoop angled inside the three rock walls that it had supposedly carved and melted back into after the theorized ice age. The back wall behind the glacier rose up hundreds of feet, steep and straight, solid, daunting granite. The back side of Granite Peak, the highest point in Montana. The top of the horseshoe-shaped glacier curved around and fit snugly inside the three rocky walls, and then in the middle, sloped down sharply and came to a straight-edged end that descended another fifty feet or so into the blue icy lake below. Straight meltoff. By the time we arrived at the glacier and sat down to rest on the rocky slope on the left side of it, I was so tired that I thought the experience of seeing it had perhaps been overrated. Permanent ice and snow with a few petrified grasshoppers in it.

Big deal.

But once I'd caught my breath and had stood to actually take in and appreciate the hugeness of the thing, I had to admit that it really was something to see. Something worth the hike up. Very few people ever had the opportunity to see a glacier this close up. To touch one. To smell the oldness of the ice. To feel the cold coming off of it like a silent shield.

Some of the kids walked out onto it and dug around in search of grasshopper carcasses.

Mr. Craig instructed them to stay near the top, which sloped down at a moderate angle and was still covered in this year's snow. Snow would provide them something to dig their toes or heels into so that they wouldn't slip.

"But if you get down there to the middle where it's angled down steeper and more shiny, that is solid ice," he warned. "It's shiny because the sun is melting the surface. You get on that, you'll end up in the lake. Nothing you'll be able to do to stop yourself. If that happens, you'll last about ninety seconds before you can't move, and nobody'll be able to get to you in ninety seconds." He looked at each teen one by one, staying his gaze on Payne just a moment longer than he had on any of the others. "Up here, it's perfectly safe. So have fun."

Safe or not, I decided that I was content to sit beside the snow and look out over the immense and rugged miles all around us. So many rocks up here at the top of the world. Big boulders. Little boulders. Pebbles. Gravelly stuff. Sand.

Beautiful perfect blue lakes. I could see all of the Sky Top lakes, and our tents beside the longest skinniest one.

Crisp clean air. The ever present tugging and pressing of the wind.

Peace.

After a couple of hours, Mr. Craig waved to everyone to join him out on the snow. He and Jacy had used the cookstove to prepare lunch.

Reluctantly, I stood and stepped out onto the glacier. It wasn't slick at all. It was, as Mr. Craig had said, deep crunchy snow. But I could see the slope at the center of the *u*-shaped glacier, pink looking, Mr. Craig had told us because of the algae that lives on the minerals in the melting ice. No warning would have been necessary to keep me from going anywhere near that part of the glacier. Any idiot could plainly see how slick it was. It forbid me from even thinking about being careless or getting too comfortable.

"What do you think?" my father asked me when I sat down beside him on the snow.

"It's awesome," I said.

"Not as cold up here as you'd think, either," he said.

"No. I guess because we're out of the wind."

"There's a glacier in Alaska," he said, "that a river has carved out underneath. I took backpackers there a couple times. It's pretty awesome too."

It sounded like it might be, but I didn't say so to my father. His talking about Alaska had a way of reminding me of all my birthdays that he'd missed, and I didn't like how being reminded of that made me feel. Bitter. Like the taste of chokecherries.

Jacy walked around and handed each of us a tin cup filled with the steaming chili her father had heated. True, it had come from a vacuum-packed bag that could be older than me for all I knew, but it was delicious. Satisfying.

I concluded that I must be hungrier than I realized, because we'd had chili for one of the meals during our second day on the trail, and then it had tasted like a brown paper bag and had a texture to match.

Pastor Adams walked through the snow behind everyone else to make his way over to where my father and I were sitting. "How are you guys doing?" he asked us, looking down from where he'd stayed standing.

I knew that he wasn't wanting to know what we thought of the glacier or whether or not we were warm enough. But I answered, "Not as cold as I'd have guessed," hoping he'd get the message that my father and I were doing well to be sitting civilly side by side.

"Well, you know I'm here," he said, pushing his spoon up and down in his chili, "if you two ever want to walk awhile, just the three of us, and try to talk through—"

I said, "I'm doing enough walking already."

My father said nothing.

I saw concern in Pastor Adams' eyes and perceived despair in my father's posture, and I regretted having responded so coldly. If only Pastor Adams had made his way over to us five minutes earlier. Before my father had brought up his adventures in Alaska.

But he hadn't.

And things were the way they were.

It would be a sin to lie about it.

Still, I didn't have to lie to ease the two men's minds. "Thanks, Pastor Adams. We know we can talk to you. Maybe sitting by the lake sometime, though? Not walking?"

He smiled.

So did my father.

Good enough.

When we finished eating, we loaded all our cups and spoons into a plastic bag which Jacy twist-tied before putting it into her pack with the stove and other cooking gear.

"Going to look for grasshoppers?" she asked me as she lifted her pack and started heading back toward the rocks.

"Nah," I said. "I'll come with you."

Jacy sat beside me on the rocks for the rest of the time her father had allotted for us to be at the glacier. We talked a little, but mostly we lay back and stared up at the endlessly blue sky.

When Mr. Craig announced that it was time to head back to camp, everyone walked off the glacier and passed by Jacy and me. Jacy nodded when her father told her to take up the back and make sure nobody got left behind. Then he ran off to take the lead.

Payne, of course, was the last to obey Mr. Craig. When he stood beside Jacy and me on the slope, he said, "I wonder what would happen if I threw a rock down."

Jacy rubbed her finger on her lips and pretended to be straining to think. "Let's see," she said. "Do you suppose it would slide down the ice and splash into the lake?"

"Let's see." He bent to pick up one of the smaller rocks at his feet and then tossed it out over the glacier.

Sure enough, it hit and slid down the snow, picked up speed when it hit the ice, and splashed into the lake.

We could hear the splash plainly, but did not see the rock hit the water because of the angle at which the top part of the glacier spread out and hid the icy part and the water right beneath it from view.

"Cool," Payne said, and selected another boulder. A bigger one.

I smiled and tapped Jacy's arm. "Have fun. I'm going to go catch up with the others."

"All right. We'll be there soon."

As I walked away from them, I could hear rock after rock crashing onto the solid ice and splashing through the surface of the water. I could hear Jacy urging Payne to start walking and leave the rocks alone. I could hear rocks slipping down the slope as Payne moved to find and heft bigger and bigger ones.

When I heard Jacy say, "Payne, don't do that," I turned around in time to see him leaning out toward the glacier over a giant boulder, trying to budge it from behind. Small rocks slid out from beneath his shifting feet and started tumbling down the slope, taking a few bigger ones and lots of dirt with them as they went.

"Payne," Jacy shouted at him, "when that thing does go, you're going to—"

At just that moment, the boulder Payne had been leaning into moved free of the slope's hold on it and began to roll downward. Payne moved right along with it and was unable to stop his forward falling momentum when the rock tumbled out of his reach.

He waved his arms and tried to plant his toes into the gravelly ground, but he was leaning too far out.

Jacy reached for him. His jacket slipped through her grasp. He fell. Down the rocks. Onto the glacier. He rolled over the snow, trying to grab hold of it and kick his foot down into it to stop his fall, but it refused him because he'd picked up too much speed.

Somehow, though, he managed to claw a desperate hold into the ledge of the snow-covered part of the glacier. He hung there, helplessly trying to kick his toe into solid ice for a foothold.

He might as well have been trying to fly to the moon in a hot air balloon.

Jacy ran out onto the glacier, where she flung her pack and made her way down to Payne. When she got close to him, she lay on her stomach on what looked like level snow and stretched out her hand.

Payne struggled to reach it, but finally grabbed on with what looked like a firm hold.

"I'll go for help," I shouted, but I hadn't even turned fully away before Jacy screamed and the two of them slid down the ice at the center of the scoop of the glacier and out of my view.

After a frighteningly still moment, I heard them splash into the water below.

Mr. Craig and I ran toward each other—me trying to tell him what had happened and him yelling at me to step aside so that he could have a talk with Payne.

"He should not be throwing rocks onto the glacier," he said.

"Mr. Craig." I grabbed hold of his sleeve as he tried to hurry by me. "They went in the lake."

"I know they went in the lake. That's why he shouldn't be—"

"No," I said. "I mean Payne and Jacy. Payne and Jacy went in the lake. Payne was falling and Jacy tried to help him and—"

The expression on his face told me he understood without me having to finish. He yelled, "No," as he stepped out onto the glacier to see if he could see them.

But the angle was too steep and he couldn't get close enough to the icy edge.

He ran down the slope and met up with the other hikers. They followed him while I struggled to catch up. Around the end of the glacier which denied us visual access to where Jacy and Payne had fallen until almost twenty minutes later when we'd run nearly all the way down to the shore of the lake across from the fifty foot drop of solid ice.

Breathless, I caught up to my father and stopped short when I saw what he and everyone else had already seen.

Payne had climbed out of the water and into a narrow ridge cut into the ice by the higher water level of a previous year. He was lying on his side, staring out across the lake, but he did not respond when Pastor Adams and Mr. Craig called to him.

Shouted to him.

I looked frantically along the whole edge of the water and all along the rest of the bottom of the glacier.

No sign of Jacy.

"He's probably in shock," my father said. "From the cold."

"Do you think someone could swim over to him?" Ezra asked.

"No way," my father said. "You'd freeze solid before you could get there, never mind getting him back."

Pastor Adams studied the rock and ice walls for a moment and turned to first Mr. Craig and then my father. "What are we going to do? What can we do? What are our options?"

My father nodded in deference to Mr. Craig to answer first.

But the man did not move. His attention still had not escaped the edge of the water and the near certainty that his daughter had lost her life beneath it.

I doubted he'd even heard the question.

So my father answered it. "We'll have to hike back up and send someone down to him on a rope."

"That'll take—"

"A good half an hour," my father said, nodding at Pastor Adams's obvious concern. "But it's our only hope."

"Let's go, then." Ezra ran past Mr. Craig and Dakota and started making his way back up the way we'd just come down.

Our teens followed silently behind him.

After physically turning Mr. Craig away from the shore of the lake, my father placed his hands on the taller man's shoulders.

"Hayden," he said, "I need your help up there. Those kids won't be able to pull him up alone, and I'm going to have to go down and make sure that rope gets tied onto him good and secure because I don't think he's going to be much help. He may not even be able to hold on."

Mr. Craig nodded slowly.

"Take a minute," Pastor Adams said, joining my father beside Mr. Craig, "and think about one breath at a time. All right?"

Mr. Craig raised his hands to his face and willed steadiness back into his breathing. Back into his shaking hands.

"Good," my father coached him. "Now you have to force yourself to think only about the one we know we can help. Can you do that?"

Mr. Craig looked ready to splinter. "I . . . Yeah, Will, I can do that."

"Good," my father said. "Let's get up there."

The three men took a few steps up the slope, but Mr. Craig suddenly stopped. "The rope," he said. "It was in Jacy's pack."

My father turned quickly to face me. "Was she wearing her pack? Did you see?"

"She threw it off," I told him, "but I heard it go in the water."

"Right. Okay." My father pushed his hands back through his hair and blew out a long tense breath. "There are more in camp?"

"Sure, but—"

My father ran by Mr. Craig and Pastor Adams, by Dakota and me, without a word. Back down the valley toward our tents.

"We might as well head up to wait for him." Pastor Adams clasped Mr. Craig's shoulder for half an instant before taking hold of Dakota's arm to lead him up the slope.

I stood beside Mr. Craig, not sure what to do. He was looking at the bottom of the glacier again.

"She was trying to help Payne," I whispered. "If we can get him to safety, it won't have been for nothing."

Even as I said the words, and believed them, and even as Mr. Craig nodded in numb response to them, I felt the cruelty of the situation like a fist in my stomach. I'd been brushing Jacy's hair and talking with her fewer than four hours earlier, and now she was gone.

It was almost too much to assimilate. I felt empty and yet dangerously full of the most stifling and horrible coldness.

I grabbed Mr. Craig's hand and started walking. I didn't feel the ground beneath my feet or the air I knew I must be taking into my lungs or the heat of the sun on my back . . . or anything until Mr. Craig and I had nearly reached the top of the rocky slope.

Then I could feel in his hold on my hand that his shock was rapidly being overrun by a much more intense emotion. He'd begun to squeeze my hand so ferociously that I thought he might be able to break my fingers, but I didn't try to squirm free of his hold.

I didn't look at him either. I didn't want to see that kind of pain or anger or panic in his features.

Soon enough, he let go of my hand on his own. My pace wasn't keeping up with his, which was increasing with the climb rather than slowing.

"Adams," he called out across the snow. "Where do you suppose we should start him down on the rope? We won't be able to see him at all, and he won't be able to get over to Payne if we drop him down in the wrong spot."

Pastor Adams stood and approached Mr. Craig. "I've been thinking about that. He was on the left side of the glacier, so . . ." He pointed to a group of boulders at the top of the glacier just to the left of its center. "As best as I can tell, that should be about right."

"We couldn't drop him over the side," Mr. Craig said, thinking aloud. "Payne was too far out." He nodded at Pastor Adams. "I think you're right."

As we walked up to the group of boulders, Mr. Craig instructed the teens to be sure, when we got ready to pull Payne and then my father up, to be behind a boulder that is solidly in the ground and to work together as a team.

"It's quite a ways to have to pull them up," he said. "But we can do it if we work together." He sat down on a boulder. "Until they're up here safe again, nothing else matters. I don't care if you bang your knees or if the guy in front of you elbows you in the head. We're pulling them up."

When my father met us on top of the glacier—it seemed like hours later but I knew that it wasn't—we wasted no time. He tied the rope around himself and started running backwards down the snow. We lined up behind Mr. Craig and Pastor Adams on the other end of the rope and held on. My father's weight didn't get heavy on it until we lost sight of him on the ice. And then there was a jerk when I guessed he'd gone over the edge above the lake. After a moment, the rope went slack. And then we were pulling. Flat-out pulling.

I did bang my knee. Nobody elbowed me, but I began to think that that might have felt better than the strain in my shoulders and arms and thighs.

But I had no desire to complain and wouldn't have been able to even if I had because I was holding my breath most of the time.

Finally, we could see Payne on the slope. As soon as they could reach him, Dakota and Ezra untied him from the rope while their fathers held it firm and then dragged him to the safety of the boulders.

Mr. Craig tossed the now empty end of the rope out and down. Then he told Pastor Adams and the rest of us to hang on to it while he tended to Payne.

First, he yanked Payne's wet jacket and shirt off. Then his wet boots and socks. Then he took his own coat off and grabbed a sweatshirt that Madison held out to him and put those on Payne.

Then he went back to the rope.

Just in time to pull again.

Most of us groaned aloud at the much heavier weight on the end of the rope this time.

"He didn't seem this heavy the first time," Rizzo said between strains backward.

"Shut up and pull," Mr. Craig snapped. "Your arms are more tired now."

Tired or not, it felt as if we were attempting to move the whole glacier.

We pulled.

And then we could see my father come up over the edge of the ice, and he had hold of Jacy!

My excitement lasted only an instant, though, because I soon perceived Jacy's absolute stillness. She was hanging from the rope and my father's arms like a drenched carpet over a drooping clothesline.

My father must have found her body underneath the water. It would be easier for the Craigs now, I reasoned as I leaned backward and shut my eyes against tears and the strain of pulling, being able to bury her instead of just . . . losing her.

As soon as it was safe, Mr. Craig let go of the rope—which put a lot more weight on those of us still pulling—and ran to his daughter. He untied her from my father and then pulled her into his arms and clung to her.

"Hayden," I heard my father say breathlessly when the rope finally went slack in my hands, "she was behind Payne in the ice. She's alive."

At first, Mr. Craig stared at my father as if he hadn't understood what he'd said. But then he pressed his fingers at the pulse point at Jacy's throat. Tears filled his eyes and relief relaxed his features. "Thank you, Will," he said.

"Don't thank me," my father said. "Thank God."

Mr. Craig looked at my father. Then at Jacy. He stared down at the snow, and then at his own hands. He fingered the gold band on his left ring finger. The wedding ring he still wore even though it had been years since his wife's death. Then he looked away from everything. From everyone. "We need to get them back to camp as quickly as we can," he said.

So that's what we did.

CHAPTER **15**

"Taren," my father said to me as soon as he'd settled Payne in beside the fire ring and the fire he'd just started, "will you go grab my jacket out of my pack? I forgot it when I went after the matches and the emergency first-aid kit."

"For Payne?" I asked him.

"No." He offered a drained smile. "I've got him inside two sleeping bags. The jacket is for me. It was cold out on that glacier."

I nodded. "Sure."

Mr. Craig arrived in camp right behind me and lay Jacy down gently beside Payne.

"Still unconscious?" my father asked him as the two men worked to zip Jacy inside the two sleeping bags her brother had rounded up for her.

"No. But she's not coherent yet. How about him?"

"He's coming around."

"Glad you had matches," Mr. Craig said quietly. He sounded exhausted. "Ours were in Jacy's pack."

"I know it. They'll be warm soon, Hayden."

I found my father's pack leaning against a boulder near the back side of his tent and struggled briefly with the straps that held the main top flap securely in place. Whether he'd pulled them too tight or whether my fingers just weren't responding quickly enough to the commands of my brain because of their stiffness from holding so tightly to that rope, I couldn't be sure. But I forced myself to slow down and focus, and after just a moment my father's pack stood open in front of me.

It felt awkward reaching into his pack. Not only because he was a man and there were men's things in there, but because these were my father's things. His clothes. His tackle box. His pocket Bible.

I grabbed his thickest fleece jacket as soon as I found it underneath his folded-up rain poncho and a flannel shirt. I was just about to pull the flap down again when I noticed a worn-looking sheet of folded lavender paper in the zippered mesh pocket that ran along the entire width of the inside back of his pack.

Slowly, I moved the zipper enough so that I could reach in and feel the piece of lavender paper. A flash of a memory teased my mind but refused to present itself to me outright. But it didn't matter. The piece of paper reminded me of something. And when I had it in my grasp, I was sure it had been there before. I slid the paper carefully up and out of the pouch and used even more care in unfolding it.

The edges of the lavender paper had yellowed and frayed with the years, but the picture in the center, drawn with crayons and a black ink pen, had not faded at all.

A house. A dog. A swing set. A smiley sun. Hearts for flowers. Words misspelled and marked in a crooked line of both capital and lowercase letters.

A birthday picture from me to my father. One that I had made, obviously before I'd started school and learned to properly form my letters and that "happy" had two *p*s.

I smiled even as tears filled my eyes, realizing that my father had carried this poorly done raggedy thing around for all these years. His only physical connection to me.

Hearts for flowers.

A smiley sun.

The words: *Taren luvs hr dady and hr dady luvs hur. Hapy brtday.*

I laughed as I wiped at my eyes and then refolded the lavender paper along its nearly worn through creases and slid it back into the pouch in my father's pack.

At least I'd spelled my name right.

When I'd reigned in my unruly emotions and resecured my father's pack, I made my way carefully between his tent and Pastor Adams' to bring him his jacket.

He smiled as he took it. "Thank you."

Dakota worked on keeping the fire going. My father tended to Payne and Jacy. Pastor Adams took several of the boys and Rachel and Madison further down the valley to get larger chunks of wood.

I saw Mr. Craig standing outside his tent, staring at it as if he couldn't remember what he'd gone over there for.

"Did you send him for something?" I asked my father.

"The pan. We've got to heat some water and get warm fluid in them."

"I'll go help him. He looks a little confused."

My father nodded. "The term is shaken," he said. "That's why I keep giving him stuff to do."

I walked up behind Mr. Craig and ran my hand along one of the poles over the top of his dome tent. "Are you all right?"

"Right as can be expected, I think." He shook his head. "If it had been anyone else's kid up there, I'd have known exactly what to do and I'd have done it. I thought she was in the lake, and I . . . I lost it." He turned slowly to face me. "Even now, it should be me taking care of her and telling everyone what needs to be done, not your father. But I can't even think what I should be doing."

"It's called being human," I told him gently, though he certainly knew that already even if he couldn't think of it at the moment. "You thought you'd lost your daughter. Forever. Anyone else's kid up there doesn't mean as much to you as your own daughter does." I reached across the space between us and took gentle hold of his forearm and was relieved when he didn't pull away.

He was shaking.

"Give yourself a break," I said. "My father knows what to do, and he's glad to do it. Everyone understands. So don't even think about it." I squeezed his arm tightly for a moment and then lowered my hand to my side again. "Okay?" I gave him a couple minutes to answer. When he didn't, I said, "Come on. We've got to get some water heating."

He laughed a little. "See? I'm standing here knowing I came to get something but can't remember what. Turns out I'm in the totally wrong place. The pan is drying on the rocks down by the water."

"I'll walk with you."

"That's okay," he said. "I'm a big boy. I won't get lost."

I smiled at his smile and walked alone back to the fire.

"How's he doing?" my father asked me when I sat down next to him to loosen my bootlaces.

"How would you be doing if it had been me?" I asked him without really thinking first.

Tears glistened at the corners of his eyes, and he turned quickly away from me to shove some more twigs into the fire.

As we sat there together side by side, neither of us knowing what to say or how to say it, images of Payne and Jacy sliding down the glacier assaulted my thinking. They'd started out on safe and level ground. Then, for different reasons, they'd ended up on the slightly more dangerous snowy slope. They'd moved down it with more and more speed until they'd hit the ice. Once that had happened, they were hurled to the inevitable crash at the bottom—the splash through the surface of the icy water.

Hadn't my life been a little like that during the past six months since my father had come back? I'd made one conscious decision against what I knew God would want me to do.

Just one.

A deliberate step off of the straight path God had marked out ahead of me.

I'd chosen to not forgive.

. . . and forgive us our debts, as we forgive our debtors . . .

. . . forgive, and ye shall be forgiven . . .

. . . if any man have a quarrel against any: even as Christ forgave you, so also do ye.

Not to mention the verses right underneath the Lord's Prayer in the book of Matthew. If we forgive others, the Father will forgive us. If we don't . . . *neither will your Father forgive your trespasses.*

I didn't need to pray about whether or not it was God's will for me to forgive my father. I didn't need to seek out advice or approval from my pastor or my mother or anyone else.

God's expectation—His edict, His requirement—was plain.

Forgive.

But I'd chosen not to.

And then one by one, that choice led to more bad choices. More steps out onto the slightly more dangerous ground just beyond the safe path. I was yelling at my mother, skipping youth group, shoving my Bible underneath my nightstand so that I wouldn't even have to see it, buying ugly immodest clothes, cussing sometimes, and feeling somehow that I had a right to be angry at God and everyone else.

And pretty soon, too soon, frighteningly soon, the ice was closer to me than the safe ground, and I'd felt helpless, powerless, to stop my descent.

But God had not been powerless. He'd watched from His throne as I'd run into Ezra that Saturday at the mall. He'd watched from His throne as I'd run from my house—to youth group—to get away from another meal with my father. He'd watched from His throne as I'd raised money for the hike and as I'd chosen my new hiking boots. The ones that hurt my feet. He'd watched from His throne as my father had driven up Hayden Craig's driveway. He'd watched from His throne as Hayden Craig had shared with me his desire to have the opportunity with his family that I'd been given with my father. The opportunity for forgiveness. For making right. For moving on.

And no doubt lingered in my thinking that He was watching from His throne at this very moment. A moment in which I suddenly longed to know how to forgive my father. A moment in which the drop-off to the almost certain death below no longer seemed imminent. I began to feel as if I might be able to drive a stake into the ground and slowly and carefully turn myself around and make my way back up from where I was sitting now to God's path for me.

I remembered the Scripture I'd learned as a child. The one my mother had quoted to me when she'd seen me struggling with the choice that had started my downward slide.

"Whither shall I go from thy spirit? or whither shall I flee from thy presence? If I ascend up into heaven, thou art there: if I make my bed in hell, behold, thou art there. If I take the wings of the morning, and dwell in the uttermost parts of the sea; Even there shall thy hand lead me, and thy right hand shall hold me."

God had reached down into my life many times with opportunities to grab onto His hand, and when I finally had, He'd upheld me. I could only thank Him that that had happened before I'd collided with the bottom of where my selfish and angry choices might have taken me.

"Dad," I said, but then Pastor Adams and the others arrived at the fire with armloads of wood, so I closed my mouth and looked back down at the flames.

My father didn't press me, though I knew he'd heard me because he'd looked right at me as soon as I'd spoken.

Just as well.

Attempting to put actual words and voice to my confused thoughts might have been a bit like putting one foot in front of the other on a balance beam across the Grand Canyon.

CHAPTER 16

Afternoon turned slowly to evening, and evening turned even more slowly to night. Almost everyone went to their tents for the night before the sky had completely darkened.

Payne and Jacy had both warmed up enough to completely regain consciousness. In bits and pieces from what they gradually told us about what had happened, we learned that Jacy had climbed from the lake first and had pulled Payne to the relative safety out of the water in the ridge at the bottom of the ice. The effort had completely depleted her remaining strength.

Payne sat up after a while, though still wrapped in his sleeping bags, and accepted one of the two plates of food that Pastor Adams had been keeping warm. Dakota asked him if he wanted more hot chocolate and then gathered the things he'd need to make some for him.

Ezra said, "That was some slide you took, Payne. Glad you're okay."

"Thanks," Payne said. He looked cautiously up at Dakota. "I'm just glad Jacy's going to be okay."

Dakota licked his lips while he stared at Payne for a moment before filling the empty cup in his hand with a scoop of hot chocolate mix and steaming water.

Not the most succinct apology or acceptance, I couldn't help thinking, but both boys seemed to be content with the other's offering. And that's what mattered.

Payne wasted no time about redirecting his attention to Mr. Craig as soon as he'd returned to the fire from stacking and covering all the packs a safe distance away from camp. Apparently Payne had been scraping together regret and courage along with the food he'd moved all around his plate in his trembling effort to eat it. "Uh, Mr. Craig, I want you to know that I never meant . . . that I'm really . . ."

"Don't worry about it," Mr. Craig said. "Everything's going to be fine."

Payne tensed at the interruption, but let it stand. "Yeah, well, I'm done being an idiot," he finished instead. "I just want you to know."

"See then," Mr. Craig said with a teasing grin that was good to see, "it's true what they say about everything having a bright side."

"I'm serious," Payne said, even though Mr. Craig's comment had visibly relaxed him.

Mr. Craig shoved a gnarly chunk of wood onto the fire. "I know you are." He ladled more hot water into Jacy's cup and helped her to sit up and lean against him to drink it. As she did, it went quiet again until Mr. Craig looked steadily at my father and said, "Thanks for your help today, Will."

My father nodded.

"What made you go into outfitting?" Mr. Craig asked him after a few moments of listening to sticks burning. "The money?"

"No. Not the money, though there certainly was plenty of it to be made."

Mr. Craig wrapped his arms around his daughter and clasped his hands together above the jumpy flames. "What, then?"

My father shifted on his boulder to fully face Mr. Craig, but not before he'd looked for a moment at me. "The truth is," he said, "I was running."

"Running?"

"Yup. At first I was running from my rotten marriage. Then I was running from the fact that I'd run from my rotten marriage." He looked away from Mr. Craig, toward the lake. "And from my daughter. Then, when I'd been told about God during a trip very much like this one, I started running from Him." He laughed. "I flew planes. I mined gold. I hunted whale and brown bear and caribou. I arranged for myself to be dropped in the middle of the tundra for two weeks during winter with nothing but the pack on my back just to see if I'd be able to survive and not really caring whether I did or didn't. I was running."

"I guess I've done some of that," Mr. Craig said after a while.

"Wouldn't surprise me any," my father said. "Most of us do at some point or other. At least when it comes to God."

I thought about my own life and nodded my agreement.

So did Pastor Adams. "But God has a way of catching up all the time."

"Yes, He does," I agreed.

"Then one day," my father continued, "I'd had it. I was at a lake by myself and I'd had it. I didn't want to run anymore. I wanted my life to be something I wouldn't want or need to run from."

Mr. Craig nodded but didn't say anything.

"So when God caught up to me again, right there at that lake, I grabbed hold and held on with everything in me."

I smiled at my father. I'd never heard it stated in quite those terms before.

"There are times I think I'd like to do that," Mr. Craig admitted slowly and cautiously, looking first at his children and then at Pastor Adams and my father. "But something always keeps me from it."

"I know exactly what you're saying," my father said. "I figured I had to make my own way. My own heaven. Or else I'd do it after I got back from my next hike, you know, when I could do it properly, in a church pew or something. Or I figured I'd wait until I was dying on the ground somewhere, but then when that happened, I didn't want Him to think I was just coming to Him because I was scared."

"You almost died?" I asked my father.

He nodded. "I broke my leg and was alone on the side of a mountain for four days before anyone found me. Every conscious hour of every one of those days, God reached out to me and I refused. 'Ah, man,' I'd tell Him, 'You don't want me. Look at the mistakes I've made. And besides, I'm probably going to die anyway, and then what good will I be to You? It's like a slap in the face if I only believe in You because I'm afraid I'll die and go to hell.'" He smiled and shook his head. "Pretty stupid, huh?"

"Not so stupid," Mr. Craig said.

"Some are saved through fear," Pastor Adams said. "Nothing wrong with a little bit of healthy fear."

"I don't know, Adams," Mr. Craig said. "Every decision I've made out of fear has been the wrong one." He tossed more sticks into the fire. It seemed that he couldn't get it hot enough to suit him.

"I'll tell you one thing," Jacy whispered, holding her cup away from her lips and breathing in the steam rising from it, "fear gets you praying."

"Fear can keep us from doing stupid or wrong things," Pastor Adams said. "It can keep us from doing the right thing, too, which is bad. But in the context of reverence for God or respect of danger, it serves a valuable purpose."

Payne set his plate aside and pulled his sleeping bag up around his shoulders again. "I sure could have used a little more of it today."

"I don't know," Mr. Craig said. "I was plenty scared today, and it didn't do me one bit of good. It turned me as useless as a backpack without shoulder straps."

"Maybe," Jacy said, "that's because it didn't get you praying."

Mr. Craig thought about that for only an instant before he smiled and playfully scrunched her hair in his fingers. "Nice try, sweetheart."

As I watched Jacy and her father, and then as I looked once again at my father, it occurred to me that our two father/daughter relationships could not be more different, and yet one thing stood out as the immediate focus of each.

Forgiveness.

Jacy was hoping and praying that her father would reach out—take the leap, the plunge, the step of faith—and accept the forgiveness available to him through Christ. My father was hoping and praying that I would reach out—take the risk, the stand of obedience to God, the step of trust—and extend forgiveness to him. In both cases, the result if we did could only be good multiplied by good. And yet in both cases stubbornness or unwillingness or just plain not knowing how held out like boarded-up and shuttered houses in a storm.

I slept outside that night. On the ground beside the fire. Mr. Craig planned to stay up all night keeping the fire going and keeping an eye on Jacy and Payne. My father said that he'd stay up too to help Mr. Craig keep awake. Since the night promised to be clear and since I had absolutely no desire to spend a whole night alone in the tent, I decided to join them.

For a long time, hours maybe, after everyone else had turned in for the night, the two men sat silently on either side of the flames. Mr. Craig boiled water, and they drank coffee. Coyotes howled and yipped in the distance, but neither man commented about them.

Payne and Jacy both slept soundly, but I could not sleep at all. I lay inside my sleeping bag with it zipped up over my head, trying to still my mind but failing.

When I'd had enough, I unzipped my sleeping bag, rolled out of it, and asked the two men if I could stay up with them for a while.

"Crazy day, eh?" Mr. Craig gestured grandly at all the unoccupied boulders. "Take your pick."

I chose the one closest to my father.

"I've, uh, been sitting here thinking," Mr. Craig said after he'd made me a cup of hot chocolate and stood to hand it to me across the fire, "that I'm pretty much willing to do what it takes to keep my hikers safe. You know, as far as me risking my own neck to help them if they get in trouble."

110

My father nodded. "Part of the job."

"Right," Mr. Craig said. "I know you understand that, Will. I guess that's why I figure I can run this by you."

My father laughed as he looked across the lake at the full moon in the middle of the far sky. "We've got plenty of time. Run whatever you want by me."

"What happened on the glacier today," Mr. Craig said, "that's not part of the job."

"Standing out of sight and reach while your daughter risks her neck to help someone out?" My father sipped his coffee.

"Right. That. That's not part of the job."

"You had to have known it could happen," my father said.

"Knowing it could in some rarely tapped into place in the back of my mind is a whole lot different than having it happen." Mr. Craig closed his eyes and pressed at them with his fingers. "Than having to stand there at the bottom of that lake and not being able to see Jacy anywhere and thinking . . ."

A gentle breath escaped from my father's lips as he leaned forward into the steam above his cup. "I can't imagine it," he said slowly. "Hayden, you know I maybe haven't been the best father to Taren, and she certainly knows." He laughed coldly. "In truth, there's no maybe about it. I've been the worst kind of father. But I can't even imagine experiencing what you did today."

"I wouldn't have helped Payne," I said with a smile, mostly to lighten the conversation. It unnerved me. "He's a pain."

"He's done being a pain," Mr. Craig teased back. "Remember?"

"I guess we'll see tomorrow," my father said, "but I'm thinking he seemed pretty serious about it."

"I think most people would try to help someone in trouble," Mr. Craig said, serious again himself. "You included, Taren."

I nodded. In that moment on the side of the glacier, I'd have done exactly as Jacy had. Even for Payne.

Of course I wouldn't have been counting on a ride all the way down the ice followed by a splash in thirty-four degree water and two unconscious hours inside a frozen ridge.

"But see," Mr. Craig said, "here's the thing. Okay, I'm Jacy's father. If I had to make or let her help someone like that, if it had been up to me—even if it was the only way the other person would survive—I wouldn't do it." He went quiet as he stared at the fire.

My father didn't press him, and neither did I.

"If I could have stopped her today," Mr. Craig said finally, "I think I would have. I mean, I'm not willing to give my daughter for someone else when it comes right down to it." He looked up from the flames at my father. "As horrible and selfish as that might sound, I—"

"It sounds like a father who loves his daughter to me," my father said.

"Yeah," said Mr. Craig, "but . . . this . . . this God you're all always preaching at me about . . . He loved His Son too."

"Yes," my father said. "He did. But He also loved the world."

"Enough to . . ." Mr. Craig looked down at the cup he'd wrapped his hands around and shook his head.

"Enough to give His Son," my father finished for him.

"Right."

"You know, Hayden," my father said, "when I first started hearing about God, I can remember thinking about Him giving His Son to save everyone in the world throughout all time who'd believe in Him and in what He'd done. That's a big number of people. So maybe sometimes we kind of lessen in our minds the sorrow of Him giving His Son because He gave Him for so many. And because He knew Jesus would rise again. And because He knew He'd be back up in heaven at His right hand again."

Mr. Craig shook his head. "Uh-uh. It would be horrible even if you knew all those things."

"Yeah," my father said. "That's what I figured out after a while. Though I imagine not as intensely as you are now."

"I guess that me rejecting Him like I have been is kind of like how it'd be if Jacy had died today for Payne, and he just blew it off." Mr. Craig's hold on his cup tightened, and he moved closer to the fire. "You know, if he'd said it was her job," he said. "Or that he never asked her to do it. He could take care of himself. Or yeah, he's glad she was there for him, but that didn't mean I, as her father, had a right to expect anything from him in response."

"You have been sitting here thinking," my father said quietly.

"Long day," Mr. Craig said, "and even longer night."

"Mr. Craig?"

Both men looked at me.

"Jesus saves us one soul at a time," I said. My hands felt numb around my cup even though I could still feel my hot chocolate's warmth. "Even though Jesus died once on the cross for all of us, we still have to come to Him one at a time. Pastor Adams told me that once. When he prayed with me to give my life to Christ, he said that if you take John 3:16 and put your name in it where it says *the world* and *whosoever* you can understand how much He loves you as an individual. Because like my father said, the world is a big number. But Jesus loves us individually." I looked through the smoke rising straight up from the fire and waited for Mr. Craig to look back at me. When he did, I asked him if he knew what John 3:16 said.

He shook his head.

"It says *'For God so loved the world, that he gave his only begotten Son, that whosoever believeth in him should not perish, but have everlasting life.'*"

"I guess I have heard that one once or twice," he said, laughing a little. "Maybe more like hundreds of times. I just didn't know it was John 3:16."

"Do you want me to tell it to you like Pastor Adams told it to me?" I asked him.

"No," he said. "I think I can figure it out."

I decided I'd better drink some of my hot chocolate before I crushed the cup in my hands and splashed the hot liquid all over myself. Remembering that verse and the moment when Pastor Adams had led me through it and then to God as a ten-year-old child, I began to taste again what I'd been willing to lay aside and silence within me in order to clutch possessively at my anger toward my father. The sense of God's goodness. The assurance of His love. The feeling of being right with Him.

Whatever I had been thinking I was gaining by holding onto my anger was not worth what I now knew I had lost to do it. And as soon as I had an opportunity to talk to my father alone, I intended to tell that anger to take a hike once and for all. A long, hard, rest-of-my-life hike to someplace so far away that it could never find its way back. So I could finally tell my father that I forgive him.

For now, though, my attention remained fixed on the man across the fire from my father and me. He was sitting at the point of decision. I knew it as sure as I knew that the moon above us was not going to drop through the sky and come crashing into the lake.

But I didn't know what to say to him, or even whether I should say anything.

So I stayed quiet.

So did my father.

And Mr. Craig. After a while though, he stood to add some newly boiled water to my father's coffee, my hot chocolate, and then to his own cup. When he'd sat down again and had placed the ladle back onto one of the flat boulders that made up the fire ring, he said, "So what do I do now, Will? How do I . . . let Him know I don't want to reject Him anymore?"

"You pray and tell Him," my father said.

"Pray, huh?"

My father laughed. "Yeah. Not something you've ever done before?"

"Maybe when I was a kid," he said. "But just as likely maybe not. And only once as an adult. When my wife was sick."

"Well," my father said, "you just talk to Him, Hayden."

"I . . . I don't think I know what to say."

"Start with this." My father took my hand tightly in his and we both bowed our heads and shut our eyes. Then, one phrase at a time, which he told Mr. Craig to repeat in his own words, he led the man through a prayer of confession of sin, of faith, and of commitment. When he finished, and all three of us had said amen, he let go of my hand and once again took hold of his cup of coffee. But he didn't raise it to his lips.

I wiped my eyes on the crinkly sleeve of my windbreaker and then, like my father, wrapped my hands around my cup.

As the three of us sat there, quiet for several long moments, it occurred to me that I'd never before prayed with someone to receive Christ. It was probably the last thing I would have expected I'd have the opportunity—or the desire—to do on this trip. And I'd done it beside and with my father.

Even though neither of us deserved the honor of being used by Him for anything, God, now that my father had turned to Him and I'd turned back, had chosen to seat us at this campfire together in the middle of nowhere at Hayden Craig's exact moment of salvation.

Amazing.

And humbling.

Mr. Craig was the first of us to speak. He leaned forward, dumped his coffee into the fire, and then watched the flames as they sizzled and steamed before fully reclaiming the wood. "I don't know about you guys," he said, "but I think I could use some serious sleep right now."

I smiled. I remembered responding with excitement about praying to receive Christ. Running around and telling everyone I could find. Hugging church ladies whose names I didn't even know. Going out for a celebration lunch with my mother afterwards.

But Mr. Craig's response, or apparent lack of one, didn't alarm me. Peace seemed to be his point of greatest need, and God had obviously granted him quite the healthy dose of it.

"Go ahead," my father said. "I'll stay up."

"Thanks." Mr. Craig left the fire and returned a few minutes later with his own sleeping bag, which he unrolled right beside his daughter's and got into without another word to us.

Within moments, his breathing had relaxed in sleep and I decided that now was as good a time as any, maybe even a divinely arranged time, to have that talk with my father.

CHAPTER **18**

We stayed in camp until almost noon the next morning. Since my father and I had kept the fire going all night, Mr. Craig decided we might as well eat a decent breakfast, and he took Jacy and Dakota down to the lake with him.

Jacy sat on the shore while her father and brother cast their lures out onto the tranquil water. The three of them stayed at the lake awhile even after they'd caught enough fish. Talking. Though I couldn't hear them, I had no doubt about the main theme of their conversation.

"They've got a lot to be thankful for this morning," my father remarked as he sat beside me at the fire.

I smiled and nodded, still looking at the Craigs. But then I turned to face my father. "So do we," I said.

And he agreed.

Eating fish for breakfast was a new experience for me. One I didn't mind at all. Since I'd gotten almost no sleep, I figured the extra energy would come in handy during the day of hiking ahead.

When we finished eating, Mr. Craig ordered us to get our tents and gear packed up while he and Pastor Adams took care of cleaning the dishes.

I smiled as I followed Jacy back to our tent and crawled in behind her to start picking up the stuff I'd need to put back in my pack.

"How are you feeling?" I asked her.

"My head feels like a herd of elk stomped over it after being spooked by hunters. And I'm still pretty wiped out." She smiled. "Other than that, I think I'm the happiest person on the planet right now. Even with all that, I think I might be." She folded her sweatshirt in her lap and then lay it aside with her flashlight and her canister of pepper spray. She looked at her hand as she fingered the ridgy edge of the head of the flashlight, but then moved her hand to her lap and looked at me instead. "Thank you, Taren," she said. "You don't know how long I've been praying that someone would say just that something that my dad needed to hear to shake him clear of all his pride and anger about Mom."

"I didn't say that much," I told her. "I think he came to that position you've been praying about mostly on his own. Well, with just God talking to him, I mean. Because of what could have happened to you yesterday."

"That's not how he explains it," she said. "Anyway, whether you like it or not, I'll be grateful to you and your dad forever."

I tried to be careful to keep from returning her embrace too tightly when she leaned forward to hug me.

"Don't think I'll be forgetting you and your dad any time soon, either," I said. "Me and my dad are going to be okay now, and you guys are a big part of that."

"God's the biggest part," Jacy said after a moment. "In and through all of it."

"That's for sure."

We worked quickly to get our tent emptied, down, and rolled up and then walked over to the stack of backpacks that Dakota and Ezra had hauled up to camp from the small hollow of rocks where Mr. Craig had left them overnight. Downhill and downwind from us.

Since Jacy's pack was gone, I agreed to carry some of the things she'd emptied out before hiking to the glacier, and her father carried the rest.

After dousing the low fire with panfuls of water until it could only steam, and then burying it with shovelfuls of dirt, we tossed the rocks we'd used for the fire ring as well as the ones we'd used for chairs out in various random directions. When we finished and hiked out of camp as a group, the place looked as pristine as it had when we'd arrived.

We walked for a couple of hours without stopping. A strange quiet hung among us. Nobody seemed to have any small talk to make and neither were they clamoring to address vocally the events of the previous day. And without any of Payne's various interjections into the background noise—howling, growling, screaming, yips, and cattle calls—nothing hindered the hugeness and serenity of the place from completely enveloping us.

The quiet soothed me once I'd concluded that there was no uneasiness at its root. So did the scenery. This was the part of the trail that we'd been hiking when the hailstorm had hit us. It looked like a completely different place in the sunshine. The green of the low alpine grasses shone out deeper and warmer. Inviting, almost. Even the rocks and jagged earth presented a less ferocious backdrop. But the sky held the biggest piece of the difference. On the way up when we'd hiked this part of the trail, it had felt almost as if the clouds and their heavy blackness were deliberately trying to smother us against the hard ground. Today, the sky seemed to reach up beyond the edge of the atmosphere until I felt that if I stared hard enough, I might be able to perceive the black of space.

But I didn't stare too long, because I didn't want to trip and fall on my face.

We hiked into and camped again, though at a different site, at Lower Aero Lake.

Late in the afternoon, Pastor Adams gathered all of us near the fire to sing a few songs, to lead a short Bible study about God's faithfulness, and then to allow us time to pray for one another and any individual needs we might have. Even though we'd had other studies during the trip, and even though we'd prayed together on a couple of the other nights, this meeting was unique. For the first time, everyone present participated. Nobody looked at the dirt or tapped their toes restlessly. We had everything to be thankful for and all of us knew Who to thank.

The night turned cloudy after dinner, so I decided to go to my tent and get a good night's sleep. Jacy was already there, and Madison and Rachel had gone to their tent too. So had Rizzo and Payne. There wouldn't be any star watching, anyway, and the plan for the next day was to hike back down the rock chute, past Lady of the Lake, and all the way out at Colter Pass. Scary. Long. And tiring.

Even if it was all downhill.

Before I left the fire, though, Mr. Craig started asking my father what kind of work he'd been able to find in Billings since moving back.

I decided to hang around a few minutes longer.

"Temporary stuff, mostly," he answered. "Nothing I wouldn't wave goodbye to in a second to be able to be up here doing what you're doing."

"Funny you'd say that," Mr. Craig said, "because I've been thinking all day that there's nothing stopping me from hiring someone on to free my kids and me up a bit. So they wouldn't have to go on every hike and could have more normal a life. As long as I could find the right person. Someone I could trust. Someone competent up here. And who understands what this kind of business is all about."

My father laughed. "Is that a job offer?"

"Might be."

I watched the storm in the sky behind my father and the one in his eyes when he looked at me.

He could do the job. No question. He'd love it. No question. He had experience. Training. A level head.

And he flat-out loved the mountains and adventure.

But the job was in Cooke Pass and on the remote mountain trails beyond it. And Mom and me and the beginnings of what he'd hoped would be his new life were in Billings.

He'd left his outfitting, adventuring, rescue worker life in Alaska to come back to us.

Would he leave us now, just when things were beginning to make sense between us, for the opportunity to go back to these things that he so obviously loved?

I licked my lips and squinted my eyes against the smoke pushing toward me on the breeze blowing over the fire.

Now that he'd done it once, would leaving be easier for him?

I shut my eyes and made a conscious and deliberate choice to deflect the fear that suddenly thought it needed to set up camp in my thinking.

Even if my father did choose to take a job with Mr. Craig and Back Trails Unlimited, he wouldn't be abandoning us like he had before. He might choose to go somewhere different, but he wouldn't leave.

I was sure of it.

"You guys would be a great team," I said, looking first at my father and then at Mr. Craig.

"We wouldn't be a team," Mr. Craig said, grinning. "I'd be his boss."

My father laughed. "Ouch. Don't know that I could go for that." A smile lingered around his mouth for only a few seconds. Then his features went tense again. "I don't know, Hayden," he said. "That'd be something I'd need to talk about with Taren and her mother before I could even start to think about making a decision."

Mr. Craig nodded. "I'm in no hurry," he said. "And it's nothing I absolutely have to do. Just something I was thinking about that might help us both out." He stood to reposition two of the bigger chunks of burning wood with the toe of his boot. "There are a couple of places on the market in Cooke," he said. "And with the increased business we'd be able to manage with two of us, I'd pretty much be able to pay you whatever you figured you needed." He sat down and noted Pastor Adams' cautious expression. He held his hands up and shook his head. "I'm just thinking out loud, Adams. Don't be looking at me like that."

Everyone still sitting near the fire laughed. Even me, though the idea of actually living in Cooke Pass or even the slightly bigger and more populated Cooke City did push a bit at the borders of what I thought I could enjoy.

Oh well. Borders could always be redrawn.

Broadened.

I had no idea what eventualities lay ahead for my family. I suspected that my parents would begin discussing their remarriage more fervently now that I wouldn't be standing in automatic opposition to the idea. And I suspected that in the very near future as a result of those conversations, Pastor Adams would be performing whatever kind of ceremony two people getting married to each other for the second time would require. A renewal of vows? An actual second wedding with the dress and flowers and the whole bit? A more simple and private exchanging of rings and new God-centered vows? I wasn't sure, but I had no doubt it could be figured out. I also suspected that Mom would be more than willing to leave Billings with my father if that's what he decided he needed to do to best support us.

So . . . who knew where I'd be in six months' time? Could be Billings. Could be Cooke Pass. Could be Alaska. Could be anywhere.

God knew. That's Who.

For right now, I was content to sit near a warm fire on a cold mountain night and enjoy the complete absence of fear and anger and confusion inside me. I had climbed back up the steep slope of doubts and disobedience that I'd slidden down. And I knew that God would uphold me throughout the months ahead that were sure to bring change.

Even if February and my next birthday found me shoveling snow off the roof of our new house in Cooke Pass, Montana, while Mom threw more logs on the fire burning in the wood stove inside and Dad headed away on his snowmobile to meet Hayden Craig and his next group of daring or insane winter campers.

CHAPTER 19

Standing at the top of the rock chute the next noon both chilled and amazed me. Chilled me because we'd have to climb down it. Amazed me because of the serenity and heart-slowing beauty of the valley spread out below us. Grass so perfectly and purely green that I wouldn't be at all surprised to learn upon arriving in heaven when I could ask God any question and receive an instant audible answer, that this had been the depth of color that covered the ground in the Garden of Eden. Creeks that ran and criss-crossed throughout it. Clean white rock. The scent of pine coming up on the wind. The sounds of the wind and of the water and of my own whispered thanks and appreciation that the God Who had spoken all this into existence cared about me.

"Make sure you've always got one foot on something solid," Mr. Craig instructed us before sending Dakota down with Rachel. "Then you'll be fine."

After a couple minutes of watching Dakota pick out a safe path through the boulders and then guide and assist Rachel through it, Mr. Craig sent Pastor Adams down with Madison. He then told the remaining boys to go down in pairs, which they did, all of them looking out for one another.

My father and I stepped down next with Jacy and her father waiting to come down behind us.

Even though I'd watched everyone who'd gone down ahead of me, I felt uncertain about the best way to proceed. Some of the kids and Pastor Adams had faced forward as they'd stepped from boulder to boulder to boulder. Some of them had turned to face the rock wall as they stepped backwards between the boulders. Some of them had gotten to their hands and knees and had navigated the whole passage like that.

I didn't want to face forward. The chute was too steep and I was sure I'd feel always like I was about to fall, especially with the wind tugging and pressing at my heavy pack. I didn't want to go backwards either, constantly having to kink my neck to see around my pack for my next step. And getting to my hands and knees? That settled too much of the weight of my pack on my shoulders, and I felt completely out of balance.

My father watched patiently as I moved from position to position but didn't go anywhere.

Afraid I'd see a little too much amusement in his eyes, I decided not even to look behind me at Mr. Craig.

But he surprised me by saying, "Take your time, Taren," quietly and in a tone completely void of anything but concern. "The goal is to get safely down."

I nodded and then looked up at my father.

"This is how I do these things most of the time," he said. He stepped a couple of boulders down from me, facing neither the rock wall nor the empty air straight ahead of us. Sidestepping. When he'd gotten to where his shoulders were level with my feet, he held his hand out toward me. "Step just where I did."

Once I'd taken three or four solidly placed steps and had relaxed a bit in the fact that my father not only knew what he was doing but was good at it too, I loosened my hold on his hand. By the time we'd reached what I guessed to be the halfway point, I let go entirely and conquered the rest of the descending boulders on my own.

"Good work," my father said when I'd jumped from the last big rock to stand beside him on level earth.

"Thank you very much."

The two of us joined the other hikers to watch Mr. Craig and Jacy quickly and competently negotiate the chute together.

"We've done this at least twenty times," Dakota told Madison when she huffed and put her hands on her hips in dejected disbelief.

"Yeah, yeah, yeah," she said. "I guess I'll just have to be content without getting good at it because I am never, and I mean never, doing that again."

"Can't be good at everything," Payne told her.

We all looked at him. He'd been frighteningly quiet since his ordeal at the glacier. Sure, he was keeping true to his word about being done being an idiot, but certainly some middle ground existed in his personality between outspoken joker and absolute introvert.

"I was being serious," he explained, probably because we were all staring at him. Like idiots. "Madison is great at lots of stuff. Who cares if she's not a mountain goat?"

"Thank you," Madison said. "I think."

"Did you just call me a goat?" Jacy grinned at Payne and smacked his arm with her baseball cap.

At first his features tensed as if in all his years of being the group clown, he'd never learned how to read or recognize humor attempted by someone other than himself. Then he smiled. Genuinely. "Absolutely not."

"Good," Mr. Craig said, putting himself right between Payne and Jacy and smiling as he looked back and forth between them at the playfulness evident in both their faces. "I think." He walked away from them shaking his head.

We followed him through the valley and back to Lady of the Lake, where we stopped to eat the last of the food he'd brought along.

"I bet your pack's a lot lighter with all the food gone," Madison said to him as he tapped the four freeze-dried-and-sealed-in-thick-plastic packets of spaghetti he'd been planning to cook against his pack.

"Forgot about not having the cookstove," he said. He hadn't had to use it since its trek in Jacy's backpack down the mountain and into the lake because we'd always had a campfire to cook over. Now, though, we were just stopping for a late afternoon lunch and needed a stove if we intended to eat.

"You know, Mr. Craig," I said, "nobody would ask for a refund if we fasted this afternoon."

He looked up at Madison and me and squinted against the sun poking down through the tops of the trees at his eyes. Then he laughed and tossed the entirely unappetizing looking packets of spaghetti back into his pack. "All right, then. We'll just push to get out of here earlier and grab dinner in town when we get back."

A vision, complete with smells as well as sights, suddenly filled my consciousness. A giant juicy hamburger smothered in Swiss cheese and fabulous mushrooms along with a beautifully red and succulent slice of tomato on a soft, seed-speckled bun . . .

"I'm going to have a steak," Madison said, leaning back and shutting her eyes. "With a baked potato buried in so much sour cream and real butter that you can't even see the potato underneath. And I'm going to drink soda and have a slice of apple pie for dessert."

Mr. Craig smiled. "Compliments of Back Trails Unlimited, on account of we lost our stove and couldn't provide the last meal we'd guaranteed."

"Do we get to stop at your place and take showers first?" Madison wanted to know.

He laughed. "I think they'd run us out if we didn't." He accepted Jacy's outstretched hand and got stiffly to his feet.

We whined a bit about having to get back into our packs again so quickly, but not sincerely. I suspected that a sudden plague of locusts or maybe a forest fire might dampen the overall mood of the day, but nothing short of that would. At least not for me. My father and I were enjoying, treasuring, one another's company. Jacy and Payne were both safe. Our youth group kids were getting along better than we ever had before. Mr. Craig had surrendered his life to Christ. And I had prayed with him when he had.

So what if we had to wait a few more hours to eat.

So what if our shoulders and backs and feet hurt.

So what if we still had a couple more miles to hike.

So what if the trail was a little rocky and uneven.

I walked behind my father until we stepped onto the part of the trail that also served as a four-wheel drive road.

Then I walked beside him.